BREAKING POINT

TAYLOR S. JOSEPH

★ ★ ★ ★
Four Star Publishing
Canton, Michigan

Published by:
Four Star Publishing
P.O. Box 871784
Canton, MI 48187
fourstarpublishing@comcast.net

ISBN: 978-0-9815894-3-5

Book design by Lee Lewis Walsh, Words Plus Design,
www.wordsplusdesign.com

Printed in the United States of America

CHAPTER 1

Have you ever been to the point when you couldn't take it anymore? When you just wanted to scream and let all your frustrations out, but you kept them bottled up inside because you couldn't let go? At the point when you wanted to slap somebody upside the head until all your anger was gone? If you have, then you're like every other normal person in the world. People have different thresholds of how much they can take before they burst. This is the story of Jim Rankin, a guy who got so fed up with his subservient life that he just snapped.

Kids are much smarter than most adults give them credit for, and some kids learn the ways of the world at an early age. Others never seem to figure it out. You have to wonder if certain kids who don't learn the ways of the world are meant to be picked on their entire lives.

There are kids who learn to stand up to opposition from the start, and others who take advantage of those who don't. These kids, better known as bullies, usually manipulate subservient kids until they learn the ways of the world. Once passive kids learn this, the bullies move on and find easier targets to pick on.

Jim Rankin was one of these submissive kids who always seemed to be picked on, no matter what. It didn't take long for the other kids at school to realize he was an easy target. It began on the third day of kindergarten when a classmate took Jim's cookie away. Jim just sat there and didn't say a word.

Soon after that, word spread that Jim was a sissy. After two weeks, he was never able to sit down and have lunch without part of his meal being taken away from him. If a teacher found out that something was going on, he would never say anything about the person abusing him for fear of retaliation. Jim didn't have a mean bone in his body, and he figured things would change for the better one day.

As time went by, the entire school knew that Jim didn't have a spine. Eventually, many of his classmates lined up, expecting him to forfeit his lunch even before the first bell rang. Some classmates went even further and made him bring extra items from home in the morning as they waited in line to take what they could from him. Jim accepted it as normal because he never knew any different, and never said a word.

As the days and years passed, Jim hoped things would get better, but instead they got steadily worse. When he was in third grade, the older boys in the school would bully him and make him do things he wasn't supposed to do, and of course he never stood up for himself. He was always getting in trouble for doing things he shouldn't have done.

It looked like Jim was up to no good, and the people who pushed him around were always conveniently gone when he was caught. Teachers labeled him a troublemaker and all of his credibility was gone. This continued all the way up until fifth grade, which was his last year of grade school.

People say the last year at a school is supposed to be your best because you're at the top of the food chain, so to speak, and you tend not to get picked on as much. Jim's final year of grade school seemed to be just as bad as all his others. He had decided on many occasions to take a stand, but never followed through with his plans to confront his adversaries. He just stood there, day after day, handing out his lunch.

The way the lineup usually worked was that Jim would only have so much to give out and when he was out of items, the person he left off on would be first in line the next day. The line would rotate from day to day so that everyone got a share. The person in line who didn't get an item would usually end up pushing Jim down or telling him off because that person had to wait until the next day. The next day things would just start over again. It was a well-organized system that a few of the cruel kids in Jim's grade had thought of. Because this always took place off school property, before or after classes or at lunchtime, the teachers never really knew the truth that Jim was not a troublemaker.

The bullies continued to get him into trouble over and over again. One day when Jim was walking down the hall, a boy pulled the fire alarm when Jim was near. The boy quickly told a teacher that Jim was the one that had done it. Because of Jim's reputation, he was taken to the office and given a one-day suspension.

After that happened, Jim finally decided that he had been pushed around long enough. *I'm going to make a stand today*, he thought, just like he had a hundred times before. This time, though, he went to school motivated to change the course of his life. He figured because he had left off in line with one of the smaller girls in his grade that it would be easier to finally take a stand. Her name was Violet and she'd never given Jim much trouble before.

Jim figured that the direct approach was the best way to handle it. He decided he would simply tell Violet that he was through handing out his stuff and she should go. When it was time for Jim to hand out his things, Violet got in line and waited with her hand out. He announced, "I will no longer be handing out my things to you people. I've had enough. You'll just have to find someone else to pick on."

Violet looked at Jim with anger in her eyes and said, "So you want to stop handing out on my day, yeah? Well, that's not going to happen, see. You better have a brownie for me today. My mom won't let me have that stuff and I'm not going without it."

Jim said, "Well, I didn't bring anything today, so you won't get your brownie." Violet's face reddened as she turned toward Jim and kicked him really hard in the shins. As he bent over, Violet kicked him again in the other shin and pushed him, and he fell.

As Jim was lying on the ground, Violet said, "Do you mean I have to go without a brownie today because of you?

Tomorrow you're going to bring me two brownies. And if you don't, your shins will feel a lot worse than they do now. You heard me — two brownies tomorrow or you've had it."

The boy that was standing behind Violet reacted the same way. "You aren't quitting now. I got your back on this one, Violet."

Another boy jumped in with, "If you think you're done, you're crazy. I'll be waiting for you every day, and it won't be pretty." Then he shook his clenched fist at Jim.

The next day, Jim felt like he had no choice, so he brought the brownies for Violet. Deep down inside he wanted to take a stand, but knew that it would be much easier to just back down. When Jim got to school, everything remained the same. Violet was in line with her hand out as she said, "Do you have my brownies?"

Jim said, "I have them," and handed them to her. Things continued this way for the rest of the school year.

When Jim attended middle school, he was still the kindhearted person he always was, and he developed a love for animals. He begged his mom for a dog until finally she got him a little puppy. Jim named him Corky because he said that he had coarse hair that reminded him of corks. Corky became Jim's one true friend and gave purpose and meaning to his life while everything else seemed to be going poorly.

Things hadn't changed much for Jim as he started high school. On the first day of his freshman year, he was opening his locker when a group of seniors walked up. One boy said to him, "So, freshman, what do you think of Riverside High?"

Jim nervously said, "I like it so far." One of the seniors grabbed him and pushed him into the locker as the other seniors helped. He yelled and struggled as the seniors locked him in.

After the boys had Jim securely locked in his locker, one of them said, as he was walking away, "Well, I hope you like Riverside High from inside your locker, because I have a feeling you're going to be spending a lot of time there over the next few years."

Eventually a teacher walking by heard Jim calling for help and got the custodian to unlock the locker and let Jim out. That happened eight more times throughout his freshman year.

Jim's reputation of being a total pushover followed him all the way to his senior year. Most of the mean kids took the opportunity to exploit Jim whenever they could. At the end of his senior year, Jim got up enough courage to ask out a girl to prom. She was the last girl that Jim thought would ever have a date. Her name was Iris and she was a real loner who didn't have many friends. Surprisingly to Jim, she agreed to go with him.

When Jim and Iris got to the prom, one of the bullies who always gave Jim a hard time came up to him and said, "So you and Iris came together. How fitting. You two are perfect for each other." Then he deliberately spilled punch on Jim. Jim got so mad that he swung at the bully and missed him. The bully pushed Jim and he fell on the floor. Just then a teacher came and broke it up, sending the bully on his way. The rest of the evening, Jim had to walk around with punch on his shirt, which ruined the night for him.

After the evening was over, Jim went home and did some soul searching. He thought long and hard about his life and how it had been nothing but one disaster after another. He felt totally discouraged. He felt like he was a nobody who let the world push him around all the time, and his inability to stand up to people made him a huge target for the world to take advantage of at will. He felt like a spineless wimp with no future. He knew he wanted to change, but every time he tried, it didn't work out.

Jim was glad when high school ended. After graduation, he looked back on his school years with regret and hoped the future would be brighter.

Jim was a fairly handsome person and grew to five feet ten inches tall. He had a thin build and straight dark hair. If not for his passive personality, he might have been successful as a ladies' man. He had been a decent student so he went off to college, although nothing really changed much. He graduated with a degree in communications. After college, he landed a job working at a department store for a major retailer. He enjoyed his job and welcomed being part of a big company.

When Jim turned twenty-seven, he decided it was time to get married. He had dated a girl steadily for three years. His girlfriend Bridget had always been controlling and told Jim what to do. She was a heavy-set, short woman with dark brown hair and brown eyes. Her pretty face was overshadowed by her overbearing personality. She had crooked teeth that could have been easily fixed with braces. She was the kind of woman who liked a man who could easily be told what to do, and she stayed with Jim just for that reason.

Jim asked her to marry him and she accepted. They were married four months later. At first, Jim's life seemed much better. He had worked his way up in his company to become a customer complaint specialist. His job consisted of taking complaints from customers and trying to resolve them without conflict. He would sometimes have to deal with irate customers and come up with a solution that would accommodate the store as well as the customer. He couldn't have picked a worse job to suit his personality, but he stayed with it anyway because of the increase in salary.

Jim hated his job at times because he had to listen to people complain all day long. At times he would just give up whatever he had to so he could please the customer instead of having to listen to them go on and on about their problems. Jim was actually one of the best representatives the company had, since the customer usually walked away happy because he was such a pushover.

Time passed quickly and Jim's wife became discontented with their relationship. When Jim was twenty-eight years old, Bridget filed for divorce. A few months later it was final, and Jim was single again. Bridget left him heartbroken and almost penniless — or so she thought — because of the divorce settlement. True to form, he allowed her to take everything he had worked for. In his loneliness, Jim thought constantly about his life and how he had really messed it up. At times he wanted to find another bride just so he wouldn't have to come home to an empty house. It was a pathetic existence, but one he learned to accept.

Over the next year, Jim went through the motions, living alone and coming to terms with his meager existence.

Exactly one year after his divorce was final, he became depressed, knowing that his life had been nothing short of a mess. He viewed his life as one big mistake with him always being on the losing end. He went to bed on the anniversary of his divorce with little hope for himself or for the future. Little did Jim know that his life was going to be turned upside down and changed drastically, never to be the same.

CHAPTER 2

The next day started just as any other day for Jim. He had nothing to look forward to and no prospects of any excitement to come. He got ready for work, filled with negative thoughts about having to listen to customer complaints for a full eight hours, just as he had for the last three years. As he drove to work that day, he thought that there had to be more to life than his pitiful existence. He felt withdrawn and alone.

Just before lunch, Jim felt frustrated because he was hungry and the day had not gone well so far. He called for the next person in line to approach his counter. He looked up and saw that it was a regular customer who had frequented Jim's station. He couldn't stand the lady because she always wanted more, more, more, and it was impossible to please her when she came up with a complaint.

As she approached his counter, Jim noticed again that she was about five feet two inches tall and weighed about one hundred and seventy-five pounds. She had dark hair and walked with a slight wobble. She had a slight bead of sweat on her forehead and an angry look on her face as if she were frustrated from waiting.

This lady must come in here once a month trying to get free stuff, Jim thought. He knew she was going to try to manipulate him again, just like the last time when she'd ended up with an extra ten dollars store credit plus a full refund on her purchase. He also knew she was a loudmouth, and he usually gave in to her to appease her and avoid a scene.

Jim said to the woman, "Good morning." She appeared to be annoyed by Jim's pleasant greeting and didn't reply.

The woman started by saying, "These sheets I bought three months ago are worn out already, and I want to return them. Look how cheap they are. Your store should be ashamed of itself, selling an inferior product like these. I expect a twenty-dollar store credit and a full refund to compensate me for your store's ineptitude and your incompetency!"

Jim said, "Ma'am, please don't use that tone with me."

The woman replied, "I'll use any tone I please! After all, it's you who is at fault. I want my refund and my store credit."

Jim replied with, "Ma'am, please be polite. Now let me see the sheets." He inspected them and said, "Ma'am, I'm sorry. These sheets look like they've been used for a year."

The woman's tone became even more disrespectful as she said, "That's the whole point. I told you I only used them for three months! What's your problem?"

Jim said, "Ma'am, you've been in here getting a refund once a month for the last year. Those sheets are used and you seem to have gotten a decent amount of wear out of them."

The woman became even more disturbed. "What do you mean, I got a good amount of use out of them? They're inferior! Are you insinuating that I would bring these sheets back after I got my use out of them?" Jim just looked at her and didn't say anything.

The woman said, "Well, are you?"

All of a sudden, a flashback popped into Jim's head about all the times he had been pushed around in elementary and middle school. He thought about his former wife and how she manipulated him and took him for everything he had. His mind was suddenly filled with a hundred thoughts of all the wrongs people had done to him over the years. He felt so frustrated that he clenched his fists and gritted his teeth.

The lady saw Jim's resistance and said, "Answer me. Are you stupid or something? Say something to me!" After that she reached across the counter and pushed him on the shoulder.

Suddenly Jim's mind and body were filled with an overwhelming feeling of complete rage. Nearly thirty years of frustration culminated in that one moment's time. Jim yelled out, "I'm not going to take it anymore, from anyone!" He had snapped. He had hit his breaking point. He came around the counter, pushed the woman back, and shouted, "Shut up!" Immediately he felt relieved, as if a world of troubles had been lifted from his shoulders. A rush of excitement flowed through his body like he had never felt before. He felt like a real man for the first time in his life.

The woman was taken by surprise and stumbled backwards and fell on the floor, right on her rear end. It actually seemed a little funny to see such a nasty person stumble and fall like that. She immediately got up as fast as she could and said, "How dare you assault me like that? I'll kick your teeth in!" She rushed toward Jim as if she were going to start a fight.

Jim's manager, Calvin Kennedy, who had heard the end of the confrontation and was on his way to the scene, rushed in and stepped between Jim and the woman, just in the nick of time. Kennedy said to the woman, as he stood between the two, "Are you all right?" The woman immediately stopped, as if a light went off in her head, as she thought about the legal ramifications of the situation.

She immediately said, "All right? No, I'm not all right. My back is hurt! Oh, my back." She immediately held her tailbone to make it look like she was severely injured.

Kennedy said, "Madam, can you walk?"

The woman said, "I don't know. I think so."

Kennedy then said, "Well, take my hand and I can help you sit down over here." He slowly escorted her to some chairs a few yards away.

When the woman sat down, she said, "Oh, my back. I need medical attention." Jim just watched, as angry as ever, knowing that the woman was faking.

Kennedy barked at Jim, "I want you to clock out and go home for the day right now!" He had no choice but to follow his supervisor's orders so he punched out and left.

About twenty minutes later, the woman was rushed to the hospital and given medical treatment as she requested.

On the way home, Jim felt invigorated. He didn't feel bad whatsoever for the woman because he knew she was faking it. Jim felt like he had stood up for himself for the first time in his life, and he didn't care about the consequences. He felt like a real man, and didn't care about his job or anything else. For the first time in Jim's miserable life, he finally had hope for the future. He knew, from that moment on, that he was never going to take any more garbage from the world. He was a changed person.

The next day when Jim arrived at work, he was immediately called into the office. When he got there, he noticed Calvin Kennedy was there, along with a corporate manager and two security guards. When he walked in, Kennedy got right to business. "Jim, that incident yesterday between you and Mrs. Catrell was one of the most troubling incidents this store has ever seen. For you to assault her was unconscionable. You could be in a lot of trouble and so could the company."

Jim should have been nervous, but he wasn't. His revelation the day before had made him a different person, and he sat there brimming with confidence as he said, "Mrs. Catrell assaulted me first and I was just trying to protect myself. She comes in here once a month trying to take advantage of the store and me. She got what she deserved. I just hope the floor where she fell is okay and doesn't have to be replaced!"

Kennedy tried to remain professional and didn't say anything for a moment. He was used to Jim being passive and was surprised by his candor. Finally Kennedy said,

"Regardless of who started it, you assaulted her. Even though we're still investigating the incident and we haven't made any decisions about who is at fault, don't you think you should show some remorse?"

Jim just said, "You heard me. She got what she deserved."

Kennedy just sighed in disapproval and said, "It's company policy never to tolerate violence in the workplace. Mrs. Catrell has already filed charges against you, and believe it or not, her lawyer has already been in touch with us."

Jim said, "Somehow, I think her attorney would have probably called you even before she got to the hospital."

"What's gotten into you?" Kennedy said, "I've never seen you act this way before." Jim didn't say anything. His supervisor went on, "You have been a great employee over the years, but we're going to have to let you go. You're fired."

Jim responded, "I've given up my whole life for this company and slaved here for years, and this is how you repay me? I'm sick of all your policies and ridiculous games. That isn't fair. She started it."

Jim felt the same type of rage as he had the day before when Mrs. Catrell had pushed him. He picked up a lamp and threw it across the room, breaking it. He really went ballistic after that and tipped over a chair and started ranting. The two security guards jumped on him in a panic and tried to subdue him by throwing him to the floor.

Kennedy immediately picked up the phone and said, "Send more security to my office right away."

Jim and the two security guards rolled around on the floor wrestling for a moment as he yelled, "You ungrateful idiots!" A moment later, two more security guards rushed in and grabbed Jim, totally overpowering him.

As the security guards were dragging him out of the room, Jim yelled, "I'll get you back! I'll get every last one of you back. Every person who has ever manipulated me will pay. I promise you that." As the security guards were dragging him through the door, he called, "You'll see! I'll get you all!"

Jim cooled down when he found himself standing alone on the sidewalk outside the store where he had worked for seven years. He stood there realizing that he was no longer a beaten man. He realized that the world would, under no circumstances, ever push him around again. He knew he should've felt remorse about his blow-up but instead he felt content and at ease. He felt like whatever charges he had to face would not be as bad as living the rest of his life the way he used to be. He left reaffirming his vow of revenge on all the people who had wronged him in the past.

The next day Jim got a call from the police. The officer explained who he was and said, "I need you to come down to the station for questioning. There have been charges filed against you for assault and battery and we need to get your statement. We know about the incident at your former employer's yesterday and we don't want any trouble with you. You're lucky they didn't file charges as well. If you agree to come in peacefully then we won't send a car to come get you."

Jim had cooled down considerably, so he said, "No problem. I'll be down shortly."

When he arrived at the police station, he said to the desk officer, "I'm here to see Detective Stevens."

The officer said, "Just a moment." Then he picked up the phone and waited a moment and said, "There's someone to see you. All right, I'll tell him. Detective Stevens will be right out." Jim just nodded.

A minute later a man came out of the security door and said, "I'm Detective Stevens. You must be Jim Rankin. Follow me." Jim followed him to a questioning room a short distance away. Detective Stevens had another man with him who started by saying, "I'm Detective Hendrix. I'll be helping Detective Stevens."

Hendrix said, "As you probably know, assault charges have been filed against you by a Mrs. Doris Catrell. She's given a statement that alleges you assaulted her at your workplace. She claims you provoked the entire incident without justification."

That woman is married? Jim thought. *I feel sorry for her husband. At least I know one person who has a worse life than I do! I would rather shoot myself in the foot than be married to her.*

"Did you hear me?" Hendrix said, "She claims you instigated the entire thing."

Jim focused back on the detectives as he said, "Now wait a minute. She assaulted me first. She pushed me and was very abusive verbally." Jim explained his side of the story as the detectives took down his statement.

After Jim was done explaining the incident the way he saw it, Detective Hendrix said, "Our sources, including your former supervisor Calvin Kennedy, say otherwise. And the incident when you were fired didn't help your case any, either, even though no charges were filed. We get people in here all the time that say they're innocent or it wasn't their fault. Prison is full of people who all say they didn't do it. The fact is that charges were filed against you and all the evidence points right at you. You're basically burned, if you ask me. By the way, have you been doing any drugs lately or taking any medication excessively?"

Jim said firmly, "No, I haven't been taking any drugs lately!"

Detective Stevens said, "Mr. Rankin. You lost your job yesterday and you're being prosecuted for assault and battery. I would say it hasn't been a very good week for you."

Jim remembered his change of personality and the vow he'd made to stop taking garbage from everyone. He said, "You can say and think what you want! But the fact is that I'm innocent! I've had enough of these games. I'm not going to say another word until I speak to an attorney!"

Detective Stevens said, "Oh, we have a smart guy on our hands. You think you're going to get off easy? If Mrs. Catrell is seriously injured, you could be looking at assault with intent to commit bodily harm. That's a felony and you could do time."

Jim just laughed and said, "Oh, come on. After she gets her settlement, she won't care about me. I know her type."

"Don't be so sure of that," Stevens said. "I'd be worried if I were you because guys like you don't fare well in prison. You'll be someone's girlfriend fifteen minutes after you walk through the door."

"Give me a break!" Jim said. "It's assault and battery, which is a misdemeanor. It's my first offense as well, so it more than likely means probation. Do you think I'm stupid? I've been backing down from people like you my whole life, but not anymore."

Detective Stevens raised his voice and threw his pad of paper on the table and said, "We have a real smart guy on our hands. Well, you can rot in jail overnight for all I care. I'm through with this know-it-all. I'm going to get some coffee." Then he walked out the door and slammed it behind him.

Detective Hendrix shook his head and said, "Boy, you really ticked him off. You have to excuse my partner. He has a really bad temper and has been under a lot of stress lately. As you can tell I'm a little more mild-mannered. Can I get you anything?"

"No," Jim said.

"Listen. I really can't guarantee anything, but if you sign this confession I'm sure you'll probably get off with a fine or something," Hendrix said. "Then you can go home right now and sleep in your own bed tonight. You'll just have to come back for sentencing." He pulled out a piece of paper and said, "Sign here."

Jim raised his voice and said, "I'm not going to sign that. I've done nothing wrong. She pushed me first."

Detective Hendrix said, "Suit yourself." After that, he called his partner back and the two detectives discussed the case a moment in private in the hall.

Stevens came back in the room and said, "So, my partner tells me you want to spend the day in jail. We're going to have to bump the charges up to assault with the intent to commit bodily harm since you weren't cooperative. We should be able to get you in front of the judge by morning."

Jim yelled, "I want to see a lawyer."

Detective Stevens said, "You'll get your call." All of a sudden, Jim became worried about his impending night in jail. He had never so much as jaywalked before and he had heard many stories about jail.

I can't believe they're going to put me in jail for a lousy assault charge, he thought. *Maybe they're just trying to intimidate me into signing a confession. They can't really be serious about keeping me here.*

After that, Jim was given his phone call. He called Brian Williams, his friend from work. When Brian answered, Jim said, "Brian, I need you to come down to the police station and bring some bail money after I see the judge. They charged me with assaulting that complainer from the store."

Brian said, "The banks are closed now. How much do you need?"

"I don't know," Jim said. "I go before the judge in the morning. They said that my bond would probably be set at twenty-five hundred dollars. So you'll need to bring ten percent of that or two hundred and fifty."

"I'll be there in the morning for you, buddy. Just take it easy."

"Thanks, friend," Jim said. "I'll see you in the morning." He was glad that he had one close friend like Brian. Without him, Jim felt like he didn't know what he would do.

Jim was taken off to a holding cell on the trumped-up charge of assault with intent to commit bodily harm. When he entered the cell, he noticed there were three other men there. A moment later, when he heard the cell door slam behind him, an eerie feeling came over him. It was if he was a lost soul with no hope for the future. But then he remembered his vow and his change of personality and he was temporarily jolted with a ray of hope.

Just a few minutes later a man walked up to him and said, "Hey, pretty boy. What are you in for?"

Jim said, "Just leave me alone." As he looked up, he noticed the man was about six feet tall with dark hair and was missing one of his front teeth. He had large, ugly tattoos on his arms.

The man said, "Don't get smart with me. If we were in a real prison, I'd have you for my slave. If it wasn't for those surveillance cameras, you'd belong to me."

Jim said, "Just leave me alone. I'm not worth the trouble, trust me." The man let out a sort of grunt and walked to the other side of the thirty-by-twenty foot cell.

Jim spent the rest of the night thinking about his life, his future, and just how he was going to get back at everyone who had ever wronged him.

CHAPTER 3

The next morning, Jim went before the judge and pleaded not guilty to the assault with the intent to commit bodily harm charge. His bond was set at two thousand dollars, and Brian was there to post bail for him.

When he saw Brian just outside of the courtroom, he said, "Thanks, buddy. I'll make sure you get your money back."

Brian said, "No problem, Jim. That's what friends are for. You should've seen what happened after you left the store. Mrs. Catrell made a huge scene. She kept complaining about her back. She kept saying that she could be injured for life. Eventually an ambulance came and took her away. We all knew she was faking. I've dealt with her before and I know how she is. Did you know that her lawyer has been at the store at least once already? He's been looking around, trying to find out things he can use in court. I think he's just trying to intimidate Mr. Kennedy. After they found out who the lawyer was, the company started treating him like a king. He was seen entering the conference room with the bigwigs. Probably trying to negotiate a settlement, I would think."

Jim thanked Brian again and said for reassurance, "You do believe me, that she pushed me first, don't you?"

Brian said, "Are you kidding? I have no doubts whatsoever." He paused and said, "Jim, I know you well enough by now to know what a great guy you are. You don't have to remind me."

Great guy, Jim thought. *Not anymore. I wish I could tell my best friend how different I really am, but I can't.* After they talked a little while longer, Jim went home to be by himself.

Three weeks had passed after the incident at the store when Jim received a letter in the mail. The letter said:

Dear Mr. Rankin,

We are pleased to inform you that we were able to negotiate a settlement with Mrs. Doris Catrell, with whom you had a confrontation last month. It was in the best interest of all the parties involved to settle out of court. Duran Corporation, Mrs. Catrell, and you have been spared the agony of a long, drawn-out trial. You will also be pleased to know that Mrs. Catrell has agreed to drop all charges against you and to keep this unfortunate incident as quiet as possible to protect you against future discrimination for employment. In addition, you will be pleased to know that Duran Corporation has agreed to pay you thirty-four thousand dollars severance pay for the loyal service you provided for us over the years. In addition, your 401(k) retirement account will be liquidated and added to the severance. You may roll this over into an IRA if you wish.

To obtain these funds, you will have to sign a release form stating that you will not hold Duran Corporation responsible for your termination. This form also states that you will not pursue any media coverage or give out any stories about this entire incident. If you sign the release, Duran Corporation will acknowledge no guilt on your part whatsoever. You will be free and cleared of any wrongdoing. However, if you refuse to sign the release, Duran Corporation will have no choice but to prosecute you to the fullest extent of the law for the incident that occurred in our office, in which four security guards had to escort you off the premises. You must make an appointment with our attorneys within seven days of receiving this letter or the offer is null and void.

Sincerely,

Charles W. Patroni

Duran Corporation, Supervisory Attorney

Jim read the letter thinking, *Great. A woman assaults me and gets a huge settlement out of it and all I get is a measly thirty-four thousand dollars and my 401(k). Here I have no job and she's probably going to live like a queen for the rest of her life. She's another one to get back at, and she goes to the top of my list.*

I should go down to the store and cause a scene. That would get Duran Corporation back. No, I can't do that because it would just make me look like a disgruntled former employee and I would definitely end up in jail. Besides that, I would end up losing what little money I would get from them as well. I know — I'll go to the newspapers after they pay me. Then they couldn't get their money back. That'll fix them. No, that wouldn't be any good either because they'd come after me for breaking my agreement.

Jim sat there thinking for a little while and came up with an idea about causing a scene at the attorney's office, but then he thought, *What good would that do? They didn't have anything to do with this at all.*

Jim felt so frustrated at the world at that moment that he didn't know what to do. The way he had been pushed around once again had taken its toll on him. He was fed up with society and wanted revenge. He had reached his breaking point again and didn't care about the consequences anymore. He was determined to get revenge at all costs. He knew his life was crumbling around him and feared that he would do something stupid and harm someone.

And then all of a sudden it hit him. There it was, as clear as day. Jim was struck with a premonition of the future and how great it could be. He suddenly had a plan to get back at the entire world, all at once. Jim knew he could never go back and punish everyone who had pushed him around individually, so this was perfect: one single dastardly deed to get back at society for all that he had been through. *It's brilliant, but can I pull it off? Will I get caught?* Jim thought for a few more minutes and made his decision. *I'm going to do it, and if it doesn't work, oh well. It can't be any worse than it is now for me. I have nothing to lose.*

Jim spent the next six days plotting and planning his revenge. He went through the details of his plan over and over again and tried to get all the intricacies worked out. He felt like he just needed the right people in the right place to make it all work. All in all, Jim thought his scheme was pretty solid and he figured, with a lot of luck, that he just might get away with it.

All of a sudden, he realized he had very little time left to call the attorney's office to make an appointment to get his settlement. He called and made an appointment for nine in the morning on the following day.

The next morning, Jim promptly showed up at the attorney's office for the settlement meeting. When he entered the room, he noticed that there were two security guards, standing one at each side of a long wooden table in the conference room. The room itself had blue plush carpeting and what looked like expensive artwork hanging on the walls. It looked clean and fresh and gave Jim the impression that the firm was very successful.

At the end of the table were two attorneys, dressed in very expensive suits, standing there and looking a little nervous. One of them was bald and overweight. He looked like he was about forty-five years old and wore a very expensive ring. The other attorney was a bit older and had slightly graying hair. He was much taller than the other man and had a thin build.

The heavier of the two started by saying, "My name is Hershel Rittenhouse and my partners name is Steven Cavanaugh. Please sit down Mr. Rankin. Then he said, "Let's get right to the point. As you know from the letter you received, this is a final settlement for your employment at Duran Corporation. The company agrees to pay you $34,000 severance, $16,212.03 for your retirement account, and $2,017 for your unused vacation time. With the money from your 401(k), it comes to $72,629.94. Please sign right here."

Jim abruptly said, "What happened to the woman who started this?"

Cavanaugh looked up and said, "We are not at liberty to discuss this with you at this time."

Suddenly Jim felt glad the incident with Mrs. Catrell had happened. He felt like it had changed his life for the better. He was now confident and assured as he grabbed the settlement paper and said, "I'm not going to sign this until you tell me how much her settlement was for."

"We can't tell you that," Rittenhouse said.

Jim grabbed a pen and held it right over the settlement form and said, "Tell me how much her settlement was for, and I'll sign it. If you don't tell me, I won't sign it." His change of personality was evident because now he was trying to manipulate someone else instead of being manipulated. He looked up at both attorneys and felt pleased with his newfound bravery.

Both men looked at each other and looked back at Jim, who was still holding the pen over the settlement form. Jim said, "You have five seconds to tell me how much she got or I walk. Then we'll end up in court and I'm sure the media would like to hear my story." He cracked a slight smile, knowing that the attorneys would be desperate to close the deal and that he had them right where he wanted them.

Jim didn't want to give them a moment to think, so he immediately said, "Five seconds." Then he began to count, "One, two, three."

Rittenhouse blurted out, "Just over $110,000. The store had to settle the suit by paying her. If the story about the incident got out, the store's reputation and its business could have suffered severely. Actually, they got off cheap. They were willing to pay a lot more."

Cavanaugh looked over at his partner and said, "What are you doing?"

"It doesn't matter," Rittenhouse said. "He could have found out if he really wanted to."

Just then Jim said, "She got a hundred and ten grand for that? Are you guys nuts?"

Jim was angry at first, but then quickly dismissed his feelings. He felt he got what he wanted by making the attorneys cave in. He knew he couldn't change the past, so he figured he would just sign the paper and get out of there and be through with the entire incident. He started signing the paper and halfway through his signature, he stopped as if to take one more jab at the attorneys' weaknesses as he said, "Should I finish or should I not?" He looked down at the form and finished signing it. Both attorneys breathed a sigh of relief as Jim pushed the signed form across the table to them.

Rittenhouse quickly grabbed the form and examined it and then said, "It's legal." Cavanaugh cautiously slid a check across the table for the full amount. At that moment, Jim felt both attorneys were a little intimidated by his presence. He couldn't believe the respect he was now receiving from merely a change in his attitude. He suddenly felt fully alive. Jim felt like a man in control of his destiny. He felt like things were going to be better in the future if he just stayed strong.

Cavanaugh said, "The security guards will escort you out of the building." Jim stood up and snarled slightly and grabbed the check and headed for the door. The security guards escorted him off the property without Jim even saying a word.

When Jim left, he felt a little angry at the fact that the check he received was not nearly enough payment for the hard work and loyalty he'd had for his company over the years. He felt that he had done nothing wrong and his former employer had let him down just because it wanted to save face and not be in the middle of a publicized scandal.

$$\$ \ \$ \ \$$

Three weeks went by and Jim had put all the finishing touches on his diabolical plan. It was planned out perfectly and he ended up going over the details several times just to make sure it was right. In the meantime, he had been putting in job applications almost everywhere. Because the charges against him were dropped and because the store wanted to keep the incident quiet, his former supervisor actually gave Jim a good recommendation. And since his former employer was such a reputable corporation, he secured a couple of fine prospects for employment.

Jim scheduled an interview with one company exactly five weeks after he was fired. He started that day just like any other day and proceeded to his interview. The company was another major retail department store chain, like his previous employer. He figured he had a much better chance of getting a job with a retailer because of his experience.

When he walked into the corporate office for his first job interview, he said to the secretary, "Hello, my name is Jim Rankin, and I'm here for a ten o'clock interview."

The secretary said, "Yes, we've been expecting you. Mr. Henderson will be with you shortly." Just as she said that,

Jim felt a little dizzy. He tried to take a deep breath but couldn't. Immediately his chest knotted up and he felt as if an elephant were standing on his solar plexus. He grabbed his chest and then fell to the floor hard. The secretary looked up in alarm, seeing him lying there holding his chest and gasping for air.

She panicked and yelled, "Oh my gosh! He's turning blue!" She immediately ran out of the office, screaming for help.

A moment later another employee arrived and saw Jim lying there on the ground. He yelled to the secretary, "Call 911!"

Jim's condition had deteriorated and when the second employee examined him, he realized Jim was unconscious. He said to the secretary, "Do you know CPR?"

"No."

"Neither do I. I'll go get help." He ran out of the office and down the hall, calling for help. In the meantime, the secretary was giving all the information to the 911 operator.

A couple of minutes later, a third employee came running in, saying, "I know CPR." Then he began to perform it on Jim.

Because of the secretary's initial hesitation to call 911, midmorning traffic, and an additional delay with the elevator to the ninth floor, Jim lay on the floor nearly ten minutes before help arrived. When the paramedics did finally arrive, they tried to revive him but they couldn't. They took him out of the building and got caught in a traffic jam, despite their lights flashing and sirens blaring, adding to the delay. As they were trying to make their way through traffic, one of the paramedics said, "I have a heartbeat every once in a while, maybe three a minute."

The other paramedic said, "Yeah, but I think we've lost him. Those sporadic heartbeats mean nothing. He hasn't had a steady heartbeat for almost twenty minutes now. He's gone. We lost him!"

Twenty-two minutes after Jim fell to the floor in the office building, he arrived at the hospital, where he was pronounced dead. The suspected cause of death was heart failure.

Jim's life had passed him by and he died at the young age of thirty. His existence had been a tiny speck in the universe, which few would ever remember. He died before accomplishing his great task of revenge that he intricately planned. He died without experiencing the great treasures of life that so many people long for, like finding true love and raising children.

All that was left of Jim now was a bleak memory in the minds of the few people who had known him. In most people's minds, he would be remembered as a person whom the world pushed around, who never really pushed back.

CHAPTER 4

After the emergency room doctor signed the death certificate, Jim's body was taken to the county morgue for an autopsy. This was standard procedure if someone unexpectedly died in the prime of life. Later that day, Jim's brother Seth, who was his only surviving relative, was called down to the morgue to positively identify the body.

Seth was about five feet eleven inches tall and had brown eyes and brown hair, just as Jim had. He was somewhat handsome, but was a little overweight, and was never really a people person.

Jim and his brother Seth had never really gotten along well over the years. Seth had always seen his brother as a spineless person and used that to his advantage. There had been many days when instead of sticking up for Jim, he would just go along with the crowd to fit in and be accepted. For example, one day when the kids in the neighborhood were picking teams to play baseball, Jim was the last one to get picked. The captain of Seth's team, who was supposed to get the next player, said, "We're not taking Jim. He can't do anything right and he can't be on our team."

Instead of sticking up for his brother, Seth just said, "Yeah, Jim, why don't you just go home? You can play when you learn how to hit, run, and catch." Then he laughed at Jim with all the rest of the kids.

Jim tried to ignore Seth over the years but never truly forgot how mean he had been to him.

When Seth entered the morgue he introduced himself to the coroner. After introducing himself, the coroner took Seth to the place where the bodies were stored. The coroner looked at the wall of compartments that held the dead bodies and said, "Let's see. Jim Rankin, right here." He pulled what looked like a drawer out of a huge cabinet and said, "Here he is. Is this Jim?"

Seth looked at Jim lying limp and discolored on the table and felt sick to his stomach. He turned away and said, "Yes, that's him." He walked out of the viewing area to the other room just outside.

A moment later the coroner walked up and said, "A little queasy, eh? I know it has to be difficult for you, but I have a few papers for you to sign."

Seth said, "You know, my brother and I were never really that close, but it sure does hit you hard when you see him lying there. I almost puked in there."

The coroner said, "After a while you get used to it. Everyone eventually just becomes a number to you. Just sign here." Seth signed the paper without saying another word. The coroner said, "He had a request to be cremated."

"I don't know about that," Seth said. "We should provide some viewing."

"It's up to you," the coroner said. "I'm not a funeral home director, but I know the cost will be significantly higher unless you cremate."

"How much higher will it be?"

"Five to ten thousand probably," replied the coroner.

"Five to ten grand? Forget it. We'll do as he wanted. You can cremate him right away."

The coroner said, "We'll make sure we do it right away after we run all the tests and after you provide us with the name of the funeral home to ship the body to."

"Tests? What tests?"

"We have to determine a cause of death so we need to do blood work and a few other things. There has to be a full autopsy performed, standard procedure."

Seth nodded, then the coroner continued, "You should let me know today what funeral home you'll be using. We have certain protocol here and I have to stay ahead of the game."

Seth just said, "That'll be fine," and he left.

Later that day Seth called the coroner's office and told the secretary that Anderson Funeral home on Jefferson Street would be the place that would be handling the cremation.

Meanwhile the coroner spent the rest of the day and a good part of the next morning gathering all the information he needed for the autopsy report. After he was done, he had Jim's body shipped to the funeral home for immediate cremation. After Jim was cremated, the funeral director put Jim's ashes into a container so that he could complete all the necessary arrangements for the memorial service that Seth had planned. The memorial service was scheduled in two days and the funeral was scheduled for the morning after that.

Almost everyone who knew Jim attended the memorial service. Jim's ex-wife Bridget was there. Seth was there with his wife. A few people attended whom Jim had known from his job, including Jim's friend Brian Williams. There was also a funny-looking man to whom no one paid much attention standing in the back of the room.

The memorial service was rather mundane until all of a sudden, into the quiet room burst a woman and a man. The woman had on stiletto heels that made her look five feet ten inches tall. She had dyed blonde hair and a deep suntan. Her body looked very fit, almost too good to be natural, and she wore makeup in a way that made her look extremely attractive. In fact, she looked so good she could have been a model or an actress who had just come from a photo shoot.

The man with her was about six feet tall and looked about twenty-seven years old. He had dark brown wavy hair and was fairly handsome. He was thin but toned, as if he'd spent many days getting in shape at the gym. He wore sunglasses, a black pair of dress pants, and a blue polo shirt. He looked confident and complemented the attractive model look-alike very well.

With everyone focused on the pair of newcomers, the mysterious woman completed her grand entrance by stumbling a little just to ensure that every eye was upon her. Everyone was so curious about this mysterious woman's entrance that no one dared look away. She made her way towards the urn where Jim's ashes were displayed.

She yelled out, "No! No! Not my Jim." Then she walked up to the urn and said, "Why did you have to die so young when we had the rest of our lives together?" She cried excessively as she stood in front of the urn. Everyone in the place was watching as the mysterious woman continued, kneeling down and sobbing, "Oh Lord, why Jim? He was such a good man. Why did you have to take him away from me?" The entire room was baffled because Jim had never been particularly popular his entire life.

"How can I ever live without you, Jim?" she whimpered melodramatically. She glanced stealthily at the crowd to be sure they were all watching, and said, "My dear love, Jim. Now we can never be married like we planned."

The mysterious woman suddenly stood up, took a step back and fainted as if in a scene from a movie. The man she was with rushed to her side and yelled, "Someone get her a glass of water." For a moment everyone just stood there in shock. The room was as silent as could be as the man said again, "Get her a glass of water!"

The funeral home director rushed in with a large glass of water and handed it to the man, who immediately poured the entire glass of water on the woman's face. She woke up and gave her friend a dirty look; part of the water had spilled on her blouse and she looked a little sloppy. The man broke the silence with, "Are you all right, Rachelle?"

The woman slowly rose to her feet and said, "What happened?"

"You fainted."

"Oh yes, my poor, poor fiancé Jim," the woman said. "How am I ever going to live without him?" She took a step back, whimpered, "I can't bear this pain any longer," and began to walk out of the room with the aid of her companion holding her arm.

As she departed the room crying, the rest of the mourners were left there not knowing what to think. Bridget looked at Seth in confusion. He looked back at her and shook his head wonderingly in reply.

The mysterious woman sat down in an outer room adjacent to the viewing room. Bridget and Seth left the viewing room one after the other, being very careful to not be seen leaving together meeting just outside the front doors to the funeral home.

When they were safely away from everyone, Seth started by saying, "Who was that woman?"

"I don't know. I've never seen her before. But I know one thing. She looks like trouble. She's not going to meddle in our affairs and get his inheritance. You know we have a deal that we'll split his net worth. We can't let some outsider get her hands on his money. Remember, if your name or my name is on the will, we split fifty-fifty."

Seth said, "I know, baby. Come here."

"Not here. Are you crazy? If your wife sees us, we're both in trouble, so just chill out."

"Easy for you to say. I just can't wait to see you again."

"Well, you just have to," said Bridget. "Now let's go inside and find out who that floozy is. The more we know about her, the better off we are."

They re-entered separately and walked up to where the mystery woman and her companion were sitting in the outer room next to the viewing area. Seth started by saying, "Hi. I'm Jim's brother Seth. I don't believe we've met."

She looked up and said, "Hi. My name is Rachelle Johnson, and my friend's name is Curt Clark. He's here to support me in my time of need. I was Jim's fiancé."

Seth said, "That's funny. I never knew Jim had a fiancé. He never mentioned you."

"Well, Jim mentioned you," Rachelle said. "He said you weren't very nice to him. In fact, he said when you were younger you never used to stick up for him. That's a shame. And now he's gone." She started to get misty-eyed again.

Seth said, "Well, maybe I could have treated him better."

"You should have treated him better," Rachelle said. "He was such a great guy. Jim and I got engaged about four weeks ago. We were madly in love with one another." She started to sniffle. "And now my Jimmy-poo is gone. I don't know how I'll ever survive."

"I'm sorry you're so upset," Seth said. "I'm just very surprised he didn't mention you."

"Well, maybe he didn't want to tell you about me until we were married," Rachelle replied.

"Maybe." Seth paused for a moment. "How long did you say you knew Jim?"

Rachelle slyly said, "I didn't say how long I've known him. I said how long we were engaged. I met him six months ago, and we got engaged a month ago. As I said before, we were madly in love."

Bridget butted in, "Hi. I'm Jim's ex-wife Bridget. I was married to Jim for almost an entire year."

"Oh, he mentioned you," said Rachelle. "He said you were kind of pretty. He was right."

Bridget, confused and not knowing whether that was really a compliment, paused a second and ended up saying, "Thank you."

"He also told me you left him and took almost everything he had and he said you never remarried. You see, Jim and I had no secrets."

Bridget said in an agitated tone, "Boy, you don't beat around the bush, do you? You say exactly what's on your mind."

"Yeah, that's the way I am. I tell it like it is. You know, Jim was quite a man and now he's gone."

"Are you sure we're talking about the same man?" Bridget returned.

Rachelle began to sniffle again. "Yes. I'm sure. Jim and I had a strong physical attraction from the moment we met. He was a real tiger when it counted, if you know what I mean."

That comment dazed Bridget for a second. In her eyes Jim had never been more than a spineless, passive wimp who did nothing right. For her to hear this from such an attractive, voluptuous woman was startling. She wondered for a moment if there was a side to Jim that she didn't know about. She knew that people made drastic changes in their personalities all the time, but she just couldn't believe Jim would. Finally she asked, "Are you sure about Jim?"

"My Jimmy-poo was nothing less than a true gentleman. He treated me with respect and dignity. Our relationship was much more than physical. He showed me how a woman truly should be treated."

Bridget was at a loss for words and couldn't stand to listen to Rachelle anymore, so she said, "Well, it was nice meeting you, and I'm sorry for your loss."

"Thank you."

Bridget and Seth quickly walked away, Bridget tilting her head to signal to Seth to follow her. When they were safely secluded outside again, Seth started by saying, "I don't like her. If she laid it on any heavier she wouldn't be able to walk; she'd fall over and die. There is no way guys like me and especially guys like Jim could ever get a woman like that to even look twice at us, let alone marry."

Bridget pushed him on the arm and said, "A woman like her, yeah? Well, what does that make me? What do you mean, 'a woman like her'?"

Seth said apologetically, "I'm sorry, baby, but I just can't see Jim with the supermodel type."

"Well, you better watch what you say about her being a supermodel. You know you're hanging from a thread with me as it is."

"Oh come on, baby. You know how I feel about you and besides, we have Jim's will to think about."

"Yeah, you're right." said Bridget. "The moment I heard that Jim was dead, I figured we could make a deal to split his estate since we'd be the only two he would put down as beneficiaries. He must have seventy-five to a hundred thousand in assets with insurance. I know I didn't get everything in our divorce settlement. Fifty-fifty, right?"

Seth said, "Right, baby."

Bridget continued, "That woman would have no rights to his money because they weren't even married yet. Besides that, I'm not going to let some fly-by-night hussy take what's rightfully mine. Now get back to your wife before she misses you."

"Misses me? Are you kidding? When she gets around a group of people she never shuts up. She would never miss me as long as she had an opportunity to talk. So give me a little kiss, baby, until later."

"No way," Bridget said. "If anyone saw us, you'd be through."

"I don't care anymore. I just want to be with you." Seth moved closer to Bridget as if to kiss her.

Bridget pushed him back. "We have to be careful until we figure out what that walking disaster's angle is. I can tell she's going to be trouble. I totally don't trust her. Now get back in there and I'll talk to you later." Without another word, Seth went back inside to the viewing room with Bridget a few steps behind him.

Bridget felt tense the rest of the evening. It was as if she knew Rachelle was going to make one last scene, and she was right. Near the end of the evening when it was time to leave, Rachelle walked by the urn one more time and dropped to her knees. She cried, "My Jim, my Jim. I'm going to miss you. Rest in peace, my love." Then she rose and walked out of the room, crying all the way.

The next morning at the funeral, in the back of the church was the same strange-looking man who had been at the funeral home the night before. Rachelle made another scene as she was leaving the church, crying, "Jim, Jim! How am I ever going to make it without you by my side?"

$ $ $

Later that day, the wake was held at Seth's house where about twenty-five people attended, including the strange-looking man who had been at the viewing and the funeral.

Seth spent as little as possible on the party and ended up serving off-brand cold cuts and a low-budget tray of mostaccioli he made himself. He spent only two hundred dollars on the entire event. Most of the food went untouched.

While people were still milling about, Bridget said to Seth, "I'm going to go ask Rachelle some innocent questions just to get an idea what she's up to. You walk up a moment after I do." Seth nodded.

Bridget approached Rachelle and Curt and said once again, "I'm sorry for your loss. I can tell you were close to Jim by the way it hit you at the funeral home." Just then Seth appeared.

Rachelle began to sniffle a little and said, "I'm going to miss him, especially at night if you know what I mean. He was a real man and he knew how to take care of a woman. I never had to do without. He was the kind of man who would give you the shirt off his back just to please you. He was kind and considerate and looked out for me."

"I just can't believe you're talking about Jim," Bridget said. "When I was married to him, he was a twit who could barely tie his own shoes. He was such a pushover that one time when a Girl Scout came to the door selling cookies, he bought twenty five boxes. I mean, he wouldn't stand up for himself even against a Girl Scout."

Seth butted in and said, "Yeah, he was a real pansy. I used to have to save him at school all the time. I even knew girls who were tougher than him. I finally gave up on him. To be honest with you, I felt like beating him up myself at times."

Rachelle's tone turned angry. "What's wrong with you? Jim was sensitive and just probably wanted to be nice. You see that as a weakness. I see it as caring. He was one of the finest men I've ever been with." Not wanting to reveal her past and already feeling that she had said too much, she abruptly changed the subject: "I've met almost everyone here except that dorky-looking man over there with the mountain of food on his plate. He must be desperate if he has to eat this stuff."

"Hey, wait a minute," said Seth. "I put this wake together at the last minute and did the best I could. The food is fine." Rachelle and Curt made faces and didn't say a word.

Bridget said quickly, "Forget about the food. I don't know that guy, either. I think it's time that we met him." She turned to Seth. "Come on." The four of them walked over to where the man was.

Bridget saw that Rachelle was right; the man did have a mountain of food on his plate and he was shoveling it in his mouth just as fast as he could. The man was about five feet seven inches tall, with greasy dark hair and buckteeth. His brown eyes didn't quite look in the same direction. He wore an old pair of khaki pants, an older shirt that didn't match, and shoes that were out of style and looked as if they had been worn for twenty years.

Seth said, "I'm Jim's brother Seth. I don't believe we've met."

The unusual-looking man had a huge mouthful of food in his mouth, so he raised his index finger to signal to Seth to wait a minute. After swallowing his food he said,

"I'm Wendell Cane." Then he turned his attention back to his plate.

Seth waited and then said, "If you don't mind me asking, how did you know my brother Jim?"

Cane swallowed again and said, "I didn't," and took another bite of food.

Seth was agitated by Wendell Cane's lack of attention to him and started to say something when Curt broke in and said, "Well, if you never knew Jim, why are you here?"

Cane, seeming irritated that he had to stop eating, put his fork down and said, "I work for Philadelphia Mutual Insurance Company. I'm the lead investigator for my firm and I was assigned to this case to make sure there was no foul play involved in Jim's death. You see, there are quite a few things about it that don't add up. I'm not saying there's foul play involved, but there could be. I'll have to wait for the autopsy report to see if any of you are suspects or if Jim did indeed die of a heart attack. Nice meal, Seth." He took another bite of food.

Seth nodded, wanting to tell off the arrogant inspector and ask him to leave. But he figured he should try to appease him long enough to figure out what was going on, so instead he said, "Eat as much as you wish. There's plenty of food left. No one seems to be eating."

Cane, still chewing, said, "Why, thank you. I'm sure all of you will be at the attorney's office on Friday when he goes over Jim's will. I know I'll be there."

Bridget said, "I'll be there."

"Me, too," said Rachelle. Bridget got an angry look on her face, but didn't utter a word.

"Now if you'll excuse me, I'll see you there," Cane said. "I have to get back to work now. This isn't the only case I have." And he filled up his plate and left, taking the food with him.

"Who does he think he is coming to my brother's funeral and wake like that and eating like a garbage disposal?" Seth said. "I should have told him off right there." Bridget nudged him to remind him to be cool; he immediately added, "The man obviously has a job to do. I'll let his rudeness go this time." A moment later they split into couples and went their separate ways without saying another word.

Once they were out of earshot, Rachelle turned to Curt and said, "I don't like that nosy jerk. I can see he's going to be nothing but a pain in the neck. I'll take care of that Dick Tracy wannabe if he gets in our way. I've got too many friends who owe me favors to let him ruin things for us."

Curt said, "Are we going to be at the lawyer's on Friday?"

"Yes, we're going to be at the lawyer's on Friday. Now don't go and do any thinking. You leave all the thinking to me. I don't want you messing everything up. I'm the brains around here and don't you forget it."

After Curt and Rachelle left, Bridget and Seth met up again just outside, waiting until no one was around. Bridget said, "I don't like that geek of an investigator. He gives me the creeps. He's just too weird. He's up to something and I don't know what. They don't send a guy like that to a person's funeral unless something's going on. I just can't believe that Wendell Cane could outsmart anyone. He's not going to take what little money Jim had away from me. When I was married to Jim, he was a complete idiot. I deserve what little money he did have, even if it is only seventy-five or a hundred thousand dollars. You have no idea what I went through when I was married to him. Can you imagine all those times I was embarrassed when he wouldn't stick up for himself? I should get that money for having to spend the worst year of my life with him."

"What about me?" Seth said. "I do have an idea what you went through. I had to live with him for years while we were growing up. Remember, I'm his brother. I deserve the money as much as you do."

"Yeah, yeah," Bridget said. "You'll get your share. We just have to find out what that Rachelle is up to."

Seth's wife Janet called out, "Seth! Seth! It's time for everyone to leave. Where are you?"

Bridget began to quickly scurry away so that Seth's wife wouldn't see her. As she was leaving, Seth whispered, "Will I see you later?"

"I'll call you. Just lay low until I figure this thing out. I don't want your wife to find out about us until after we get the money. Now go."

Seth went to his wife, who began to talk at a rapid pace as she always did. "Where were you? Our guests are leaving. I was talking to an old friend for an hour and did we ever catch up!" Before Seth could say a word, Janet continued, "Now, come with me. We need to see our guests off. You know, you should be more sociable, like me. If you were, you'd be much happier, like me."

Seth sighed at her never-ending talking and said, "Yes, dear," and followed her to see everyone off. He wanted to blurt out the news about leaving her and going with

Bridget, but he knew he couldn't. He knew Bridget would have a fit if he told his wife about them before they had their hands on Jim's money, and the last thing Seth wanted was to make Bridget mad. Seth kept encouraging himself by thinking, *Just a little while longer and I won't ever have to listen to her again.*

CHAPTER 5

Friday came quickly and it was time for everyone to meet at the attorney's office to hear Jim's will. Bridget and Seth were seated at the end of a long wooden table that spanned the length of the twenty-by-twenty-foot plush office. When Rachelle and Curt walked in, they sat down at the other end of the table. Janet waited out in the car because she said she didn't have the stomach for legal matters. A moment later, Jim's best friend Brian walked in and sat between the two couples in the middle of the room. And of course Wendell Cane was there, sitting off to the side looking as obnoxious as he had before.

When the attorney entered the room he said, "My name is Stephen Pelewski. I wrote Jim's will and I'll be overseeing his last wishes. I know you expect me to read his last will and testament like in the movies, but that isn't going to happen. His will was notarized and is perfectly legal. You'll all get a copy of it before you leave. I'll just go over the specifics and explain exactly what he wanted.

"First of all, I would like to say to all of you that I'm sorry for your loss. Even though I only knew Jim for a brief period of time, I can say I haven't met a nicer man. He had a genuine way about him that few people have." The attorney shuffled some papers and said, "First of all, Jim's possessions with his bank account and with his other investments equate to approximately one hundred and fifteen thousand dollars. This is a conservative estimate and could actually be a little higher when everything is all said and done."

Bridget looked over at Seth as if to say *I told you he had money stashed away.*

The attorney went on, "Jim's wishes were as follows: To my dear friend Brian Williams, I want to thank you for being such a great friend and for always being there for me. If it weren't for you I would have given up on life a long time ago. I'm leaving you twenty-five thousand dollars.

"To my ex-wife Bridget, who put me through the worst year of my life, I leave nothing. To my brother Seth, who treated me like dirt my entire life, I also leave nothing. And to my lovely fiancée Rachelle, I leave the bulk of my estate, including my insurance policy."

Bridget yelled, "There must be some kind of mistake! When I was married to Jim, I was the sole beneficiary of his estate."

Jim's lawyer said, "This is true. Jim changed that a short time ago, after he was fired. I personally drew up the papers. It's perfectly legal."

Bridget bellowed, "You mean to tell me I was married to him for the worst year of my life and I get nothing? That will has to be bogus."

Seth blurted out, "You think it's bad you get nothing? I put up with that loser my entire life. I even paid for his funeral and I don't even get reimbursed. Well, we shall see about that. You'll be hearing from my attorney."

Jim's attorney said, "Yes. Go ahead and spend as much as you want. You're going to end up with nothing. There isn't a court in the world that's going to change this will. You're just going to have to deal with things the way they are. Maybe you should have been nicer to Jim when he was alive."

Wendell Cane butted in and said, "I'm afraid he's right."

Jim's attorney followed with, "I'm sure all of you know Wendell Cane by now."

Cane continued, "Yes, I've met everyone already. I see that shortly after Jim Rankin died, all anyone cares about is his money. That's typical."

Bridget looked as though she was gearing up to tell Cane off. Cane beat her to the punch by saying, "About four weeks ago, Jim took out a sizable insurance policy on himself. The insurance policy was for five million dollars. Pending my investigation, it could be paid out in thirty to ninety days."

Everyone's jaws dropped and their eyes widened. Cane went on to say, "I find it very unusual that Jim dropped dead less than a month after finalizing the policy. I'll be investigating his death just to make sure there's no fraud involved."

Seth gulped and caught his breath as he said, "Who is the beneficiary on the policy?"

"The sole beneficiary is Rachelle Johnson, for the entire five million."

Rachelle looked dizzy as she said, "You are serious, aren't you?"

"I don't joke when it comes to money," said Cane.

"I had no idea. I mean, I signed a lot of papers, but Jim never said anything. I don't feel so well."

Jim's attorney said, "Please make yourself comfortable, Ms. Johnson. In the event that Rachelle is unable to accept the money, it will be split between Seth Rankin, Bridget Bartkowski and Brian Williams. That provision was in the will and in the policy."

Bridget burst out, "Five million dollars! That's not right. It should be mine. I suffered the most."

Jim's attorney interjected, "Well, it isn't yours. Obviously he thought very highly of Rachelle. Those were his wishes. Now if you will excuse me, I have to be in court in thirty minutes. If you have any questions, you can call the office. We'll be in touch if there are any further developments."

Cane spoke up, "I will definitely be in touch with each one of you to ask questions and to complete my investigation. You see, whenever there is a policy of this size, my company requires a thorough investigation. Philadelphia Mutual is not in the habit of paying out a policy that size unless they are absolutely sure it's warranted."

Rachelle said, "Warranted, what do you mean warranted? My Jim is dead and all you can think about is money.

What kind of person are you? It should be as clear as day to you that I loved him and never would hurt him."

Cane abruptly said, "Until I see an autopsy report I won't know anything. I'm not saying you'd be involved with any foul play, but people have been known to do some dastardly things to get that kind of money. Also, with the body being cremated before I could see it, it's a little more suspicious."

He paused and continued, "There are a few other unanswered questions that I don't want to get into right now. If everything is normal then we don't mind paying out the money. We have to be absolutely sure. And besides, the terms of the policy give the company up to ninety days."

Rachelle said, "Ninety days." Then she realized that Cane was going to be mostly investigating her and she said, "I guess ninety days isn't that long. In the meantime, I wonder how long it will take to transfer the rest of the estate to me."

Jim's attorney, apparently aggravated, replied, "You should get forty thousand in cash within a week or two. The rest you should get in about three to six months after everything is sold at auction. You can take his personal belongings from his apartment at your convenience. The things at his apartment don't have much value. They're mostly sentimental items. His assets will be liquidated and you will hear from us very soon."

Rachelle said, "I guess that'll do."

Cane took his leave, saying again, "Don't forget: I'll be in touch."

Seth and Bridget stormed out of the room leaving Rachelle, Curt and Brian behind with Cane. Once outside, Bridget clenched her fists in anger. She was about to speak to Seth, then realized Seth's wife was watching from the car. "We'll talk about this later," she said, and left.

Rachelle and Brian, having wrapped things up by signing papers with the attorney's secretary, took their leave as well. Outside, Rachelle said, "Yes! Five million dollars! I knew that idiot Jim would lead to a big payday. I just didn't realize he was going to leave me five million dollars. And all we have to do is wait ninety days. Yes! My ship has come in! We're rich!"

"What about that nosy investigator Cane?"

"As far as I'm concerned, he doesn't have anything on us. You know I have connections at the police department and by this time tomorrow I'll know everything about him. He and his company are going to have to pay me that money. I'm going to see to it that they don't worm out of it. I've been waiting my whole life for something like this and no one, I mean no one, is going to get in my way."

Curt said, "Yeah. I think Cane might be a little smarter than he looks, though."

"You leave all the thinking to me. You just do what you're told and don't screw anything up. Besides, who am I to question the fact that Jim left me as the sole beneficiary of his insurance policy? I didn't even know about it."

"What about Bridget and Seth? They seem like greedy little creeps, and they're second in line, you know."

"Yeah, they could be a problem." Rachelle said. "They'd better not try anything. She seems like a conniving loudmouth and he seems so full of himself that he would do anything to get that money. I don't trust them one bit. I'm going to get a handgun and carry it with me at all times. If either of them tries anything, I'll put a bullet right in their head. As I said before, I'm not letting anyone get in my way. This is a dream come true and they're not going to mess it up." And with that, they went back to Rachelle's house.

$ $ $

The next morning, Cane started his investigation by going to the office where Jim had dropped dead. At the receptionist's desk, he explained who he was and asked to talk to the secretary who was there when Jim collapsed. After being escorted to the secretary's desk, he introduced himself and gave her one of his cards.

Cane noticed that she was about twenty-five years old and quite pretty. He started by saying, "As you know, I am investigating the death of the man who died here a few days ago."

The secretary said, "Yes, what a tragedy. He was so young to die like that. It really shook me up."

"I'll bet it did. Can you tell me exactly what happened?" Cane said.

"There isn't really anything to tell that I didn't tell the police. When Mr. Rankin went to sign in for the job interview, he fell to the floor and passed out. I went to go get help and called 911. They did CPR on him until the ambulance came and that was it. I did everything I could."

Satisfied, Cane said, "If you think of anything else, call me."

The secretary looked at Cane's card again and said, "All right."

Cane thanked her and left. He thought it was best to visit the paramedics next, and drove over to the fire station that had responded to the call; he knew most of the fire commanders in the city because he had worked closely with them on arson cases before.

When Cane walked into the station, Commander Lepere was in his office doing his paperwork and scheduling for the week. Cane walked into Lepere's office and extended his hand for a handshake.

Lepere shook his hand and said, "So what brings you to these parts?"

Cane responded, "That dead-on-arrival a few days ago who dropped dead at the office building had a five-million-dollar policy on him. I'm on the case. The body was cremated and we just want to tie up all the loose ends."

"Talk about luck," said Lepere. "Who's the beneficiary?"

"His girlfriend. They weren't even married. It looks legitimate so far."

"Well, it's your lucky day; the two paramedics who tried to resuscitate him just started their shift. They're in the kitchen. Feel free to go talk to them. Do you think you'll have to pay this one out?"

"It looks like it. I just want to check out a couple of things that don't add up."

"Well, good luck to you. And tell Dunlop and Carnes to come in here after they're done talking with you." He started shuffling papers around again, and without another word, Cane headed for the kitchen.

Dunlop and Carnes were eating lunch. When they saw Cane, they stopped eating and shook his hand. Even though Cane was unusual-looking and eccentric, he had the respect of many of the firefighters and police because it was as if they were on the same team.

Cane started by saying, "I'm investigating that DOA at the office building you had recently. The guy's name was Jim Rankin. You do remember him, don't you?"

"Yeah, I remember," Dunlop said. "Those ones aren't easy to forget. He was in the prime of his life. What a shame."

"Well, he had a five million dollar policy on him."

Carnes said, "Wow! Five million! That's a lot of money. If I had five million I'd move to Hawaii."

"Yeah," Cane said. "I just want to make sure everything is on the up-and-up. When you guys got to the scene, was he coherent?"

"No. He was out," Dunlop said. "We did CPR on him and he didn't respond, so we did immediate transport. We tried to revive him on the way, but no dice. We even tried to shock him with the paddles, but that didn't work either. He was recorded as a DOA."

"I see. Don't you find it a little unusual for a man in the prime of his life like that to have a heart attack?"

Carnes said, "It's a little unusual, but we've seen it before."

"Is there anything else that I should know?"

Dunlop thought a moment and said, "Well, it's probably nothing, but on the way to the hospital an unusual thing happened. Rankin was actually clinically dead by then, but I thought every once in a while I would get a faint heartbeat. Maybe like five beats a minute. Of course that's impossible. No one could survive with five beats a minute.

The beats were so faint that my equipment didn't even pick them up; I thought I got them when I took his pulse. It was weird. They weren't consistent and I wasn't even sure I got them, so I just let it go. He was pronounced dead at the hospital anyway."

"That is weird," Cane said. "Have you ever seen anything like that before?"

Dunlop said, "Well actually on rare occasions people's hearts have stopped for up to twenty minutes or longer and then all of a sudden they have a heartbeat. Almost always they die though. We've never had anyone survive after that long. I must have been mistaken."

"Yeah I've heard about people being brought back after they were clinically dead, but you're probably right about this one," Cane said. He thanked the paramedics, told them that Lepere wanted to see them in his office, and then left. He still felt a little curious about how the paramedics had thought they had a faint heartbeat once in a while, so he decided to pay the emergency room doctor a visit.

Cane called the hospital and found that the doctor who was on duty when Jim arrived was ending his shift in an hour; he decided to go there and wait for him. At the hospital, he was led into a simple office with a desk and three chairs and a few diplomas on the walls. After a twenty-minute wait, the doctor walked in and said, "Hello, I'm Dr. Harris. How can I help you?"

Part of Cane's job was to observe people and draw conclusions from the way they behaved, so he noticed that the doctor appeared to be about fifty years old, was of medium height, and had slightly graying hair. He was slightly overweight, probably from the long hours he put in on the job and the lack of exercise from having such a demanding position.

Cane introduced himself and said, "I'm investigating Jim Rankin's death. You do remember Jim Rankin, don't you?"

"I remember him. Hang on a second. Let me pull his file." Dr. Harris went to a file cabinet and shuffled through some papers. "I keep a duplicate file on all patients who die in the emergency room on my shift. With the way the public is about filing law suits, you have to." After a second he said, "Oh yes, I remember it clearly now. He had a heart attack at just thirty years of age. He was gone when he arrived."

Cane asked, "Are you sure he was dead on arrival? The paramedics claim they might have had a heartbeat once in a while, maybe five a minute."

"Are you kidding me? I've been in this business for twenty-five years. I know a DOA when I see one. Besides, I examined him personally. He was dead all right. It couldn't have helped taking almost twenty minutes to get him here, either. He was long gone. I don't even know why I'm having this conversation with you. You can't really be questioning whether he was dead or not?"

Cane explained, "It's just that he had a five million dollar policy on him and he died right after he took it out."

"Listen," said Dr. Harris. "As far as the paramedics thinking that they got a slight heartbeat, they could have been mistaken. You see, the body functions long after it's dead. If you talk to the coroner, you'll find out that it isn't uncommon for a body to make a sudden jerk many hours after it's clinically dead. A cadaver is filled with a little excess air after they are long gone. Many times a body will release this air with a little movement long after the person is dead, so the paramedics could have thought they got a heartbeat when in reality they actually didn't. All I know is he was dead on arrival and I don't make mistakes when it comes to a man's life."

Cane stated, "The paramedics said on rare occasions people will get a sudden heartbeat even up to twenty minutes after they're heart stopped. I've also heard stories where people were revived even after excessive periods of time."

"It's true a few people have survived after not having a heartbeat for twenty or thirty minutes, but that's so rare, one in a million." Dr. Harris said. "I even heard one time when a boy fell through the ice on a pond and was submerged for almost an hour. They brought him back. That's divine intervention as far as I'm concerned."

Cane said, "So you're sure?"

"Boy, you sure are aggravating," said Dr. Harris in a disturbed tone. "I signed the death certificate, didn't I? You people are all alike. I've been a physician for twenty-five years and he was clinically dead. As much as it is going to hurt you, it looks like you'll have to pay out on this one."

Disturbed at the doctor's attempt to berate him, Cane nevertheless continued, "One more thing. Was it really busy that day?"

"It's busy here every day. I had another heart attack victim that day as well as a car accident with three people injured. It was a madhouse, just as it usually is."

"I see," Cane mumbled.

Dr. Harris said, "Now if you'll excuse me, I have to go home and get some rest. I have to be back here in just over twelve hours."

Cane thanked the doctor and left. He had been in this business a long time so he knew his next stop had to be the police station. When he got there, he approached the front desk officer, whose name was Brent Crosby. Cane leaned over Crosby's desk and said, "Is Munson here?"

Crosby smiled and said, "All right, you slimy son of a gun. What do you want? Man, you get uglier every time I see you. If I was a woman and I saw you, I'd run the other way."

"I'm surprised you're still here," Cane said.

"What do you mean, you're surprised I'm still here? Have you heard anything about budget cuts?"

Cane had been through the same playful routine with Crosby many times before and usually had a great come-back. Cane and Crosby always joked around and enjoyed each other's wit. "No. I just figured you'd be down at the donut shop right now. Haven't you usually had six or eight donuts by this time of day?"

Crosby smiled and said, "Yeah, whatever."

After a few minutes of laughing and catching up, Cane repeated, "Is Munson in?"

Crosby said, "He's in. Go on back."

Cane walked back to Detective Munson's office. Cane and Munson went back a long way. They had both been involved in a case when Cane first started working at Philadelphia Mutual twenty years before. In fact, Cane had played a pivotal role in solving quite a few cases for the detective. Munson revered Cane as a worthy investigator, and since he was the lead detective, he gave Cane the freedom to come see him at will.

Detective Munson was six feet tall and was about forty-six years old. He had a larger-than-average, muscular build and brown thinning hair with a touch of grey. He wore his standard attire — dress pants, a shirt and tie, and glasses.

He saw Cane and said, "Hey, Cane, how've you been?" and shook his hand.

"I've been fine; how about you, Dennis?"

"Same old thing. I'm just trying to balance work and home and still remain sane. Sometimes I wonder if being the lead detective is really worth the aggravation for the little bit of extra money they pay me."

"Yeah, we all have our crosses to bear."

After they exchanged a few pleasantries, Cane said, "I'm working on a case where some guy named Jim Rankin had a five million dollar policy out on him. He suddenly dropped dead a few days ago."

Munson said, "Yeah, I know all about that guy. He dropped dead at a job interview. I'm waiting for the autopsy report to determine the cause of death. I don't think there was any foul play."

"I was hoping you could run a check on five people for me. They're an unusual bunch and I want to be sure they weren't involved in Rankin's death."

"Let me see the list." Cane handed Munson the list, which featured Rachelle, Curt, Bridget, Seth and Brian.

"I don't know why," said Cane, "but I have a funny feeling these people are hiding something."

Munson laughed. "You always think everyone is hiding something."

Cane laughed too. "Most people are hiding something, aren't they? That's what makes me such a great investigator. No one is above suspicion."

Munson eyeballed the list and said, "This time it's really going to cost you."

Cane put his hand out to signal, *how much?* Munson said, "Lunch from the Sub Shack with dessert."

Cane nodded and said, "The usual?"

"Yep, Italian sub with extra cheese and extra mayo and three chocolate chip cookies."

"Done! It'll be here in half an hour."

"Fine. You can pick up your rap sheets at five."

"Thanks."

He left and called the Sub Shack on the way out of the building to make sure Munson's lunch would be delivered.

Next, he planned to interview Brian Williams. Cane thought it best to try to get some dirt on the others involved from Brian before questioning them. Cane went to Jim's old workplace where Brian was still employed. He went to Jim's former supervisor Calvin Kennedy and explained the situation to him, asking if he could ask Brian a few questions.

Kennedy said, "You know, we have a business to run and I don't think that would be appropriate."

"Well, I'm trying to keep this as quiet as possible to avoid any attention. You don't want any attention about this, do you? I mean, after all, you did fire a man and he ended up dead shortly after he was let go."

Kennedy thought for a second and said, "You know, you're right." He called his secretary and told her to have Brian Williams sent up to his office as soon as possible.

Cane didn't want to waste a moment so he quickly said, "While we're waiting, I was wondering if you wouldn't mind answering a few questions as well?"

Kennedy nervously said, "No, not at all."

"Did Jim ever drink at work?"

"Absolutely not. I would've known if something like that was going on during my shift. Jim was a perfect employee. Did you know he hadn't missed a day or been late in years? Yeah, he was perfect until he snapped and went off on that lady." He explained the entire incident from his perspective and added, "You know, for what it's worth, I never thought Jim would blow up like that."

Just then there was a knock at the door, and Brian walked in.

Cane turned to Kennedy and said, "I would like to question Brian alone, if you don't mind."

Kennedy nodded. "You can use the conference room right next door; follow me."

Cane and Brian followed Kennedy to the conference room and, as soon as Kennedy left, Cane got right to the questioning.

"How long did you know Jim Rankin?"

"About seven years. We were good friends, but not like best friends."

"Define good friends compared to best friends."

"Well, we hung out at work all the time and went places like the movies together once in a while, but not all the time."

"How was he as a worker?"

"He was the best. I still don't understand why he snapped that day. It didn't make sense."

Cane asked, "How long have you known his fiancée Rachelle?"

"I didn't. She was as much of a surprise to me as everyone else."

"Let me get this straight. Your friend gets engaged to a woman and takes out a five million dollar insurance policy with her as the beneficiary and he never even mentioned any of it to you? Don't you find this strange?"

"It is weird, isn't it?"

Cane continued, "Tell me about his ex-wife."

"Bridget is a waste of space. Jim was good to her and treated her like a queen. So what if he was passive-aggressive? She still shouldn't have done that to him."

Puzzled, Cane asked, "Done what?"

"Well, about six months after Jim and Bridget were married, Jim came home early from work and found Bridget with another man. It was one of their neighbors in their apartment building. Jim was shattered, the poor guy. I felt so bad for him. Jim ended up forgiving Bridget and trying to work things out. Two weeks later, Jim found her with a different man. This time it was someone she knew before they were married. Jim was furious but still wanted to try and work things out. Can you believe he didn't dump her right then and there?"

"Why didn't he divorce her after that?" Cane said.

"Jim was so forgiving that he gave her another chance. Bridget ended up leaving him about three months later and filing for divorce. In the process she took him to the cleaners. She is true pond scum. That's why I was glad when I found out she didn't get any more of his money."

"And what about you? You're one of the group that is second in line to get the insurance payout. How do you feel about that?"

"It really doesn't matter to me," Brian said. "I don't care about it. Let all of his miserable relatives fight over it."

Brian seemed sincere, but Cane knew that he should never rule anything out because things aren't always as they seem. Cane thanked Brian for the information and left.

It's time to stir things up a little. I'm going to go talk to Bridget. She's probably chomping at the bit over Rachelle being named beneficiary, thought Cane as he was leaving. He decided to stake out Bridget's house first before approaching her; this way he could see what she was up to, if anything.

Cane had waited less than an hour when Seth showed up. Cane carefully watched from a distance with his binoculars while the two sat down and started talking on Bridget's front porch. As an insurance investigator, Cane didn't follow all of the rules that the police did; he usually had a total lack of concern about privacy rights. He seldom cared about the way people felt as long as he learned the truth. His main goal was always to prove his case.

He pulled out a device that looked like a small satellite dish. It allowed him to hear conversations from a distance without anyone knowing that he was listening. Cane put a small earphone in his ear and aimed the device directly toward Bridget and Seth. Instantly he heard Bridget say, "That's enough now."

Seth tried to kiss Bridget. "Come on, honey. You know I'm crazy about you."

Bridget firmly pushed Seth away. "Not now! We have that witch Rachelle to deal with and I will not let her get in the way of what's rightfully mine. We have to figure this out. Give me a day or two and I'll call you. Did you hear me? Give me a day or two and I'll call you."

Seth just said, "Oh, baby. I have to wait two days?"

"Yes, you do," Bridget said. "You know if your wife finds out about us, things are going to get crazy and I don't need that right now. Now go home before she gets suspicious."

As Seth left, Cane murmured, "Very interesting."

After another fifteen minutes, Bridget got in her car and left. Cane followed her to a park near her house, where she met a different man. Cane was hoping that if anything did happen to Rachelle and Bridget was involved, then his company would have a loophole to let them avoid at least her part of the payout.

Cane carefully positioned himself a quarter of a block away from Bridget and the man, so as to remain unseen but still hear their conversation with his device. He saw through his binoculars that the man was handsome, a few years younger than Bridget and of medium height, with dark straight hair that half covered his ears.

As Cane watched and listened, Bridget reached over and kissed the man, and said, "Rick, I love you and I missed you so much. I can't wait until we get that five million. Then we'll be in the Caribbean home free, just you and me on the beach with the warm breeze blowing through our hair. I can't wait."

"First we have to take care of that gold-digger Rachelle," Rick said.

Cane muttered, "This just keeps getting better all the time." Bridget and Rick sat there kissing and talking for a few minutes. When they left, Cane followed them to Rick's apartment.

A few minutes later, Bridget left Rick's apartment and drove away. Cane shook his head in wonder. *I can't believe how complicated these people's lives are. They have no respect for other people and it seems like they would cut each other's throats for that money. No one is loyal and no one can be trusted.*

It was getting to be late afternoon so Cane figured that he had spent enough time staking out Bridget. He figured his next move was to go see the coroner.

When he arrived at the county morgue, the place seemed all too familiar to him. He had worked on cases before involving death and his path always took him there. Cane knew people found him eccentric, but most people found the coroner downright weird. Every time Cane left the morgue, he always felt glad for the job he had and was relieved he didn't have to deal with doing autopsies.

Cane went to the front desk and said, "I'm here to see Jake. He's expecting me."

The clerk said, "Go on back. He told me you would be coming." Cane walked through a set of double doors and back through the morgue. Just as he reached Dr. Jake Hutchinson's office, he heard a voice that sounded like Dr. Hutchinson on the phone.

Cane waited just outside the office so as not to disturb the hardworking doctor. He heard him say, "I'll have your money in a week. Don't worry, I'm good for it. I know I owe you five grand. I'll have it in a week. No, don't send anyone down here. You know I'm a well-respected part of the community. If someone sees your people here, both you and I could be ruined. I'll have it in a week. In the meantime, put a thousand on the Knicks tonight minus four points at home."

The person on the other line must have said something, because Dr. Hutchinson paused for a moment and said, "Just take the bet. I'm good for it. Yes I'm sure, on the Knicks to cover. That's right, one grand. It's a sure thing. All right, one week. You know I'll have it. Thanks. I'll talk to you later."

Dr. Hutchinson hung up, walked out of his office and saw Cane. He asked, "How long have you been standing there?"

"Just a minute or two."

"Did you hear my entire conversation?"

"Don't worry about it. It's fine." Cane cracked a smile; he knew that if he ever needed a favor in the future he had it coming from the doctor. Knowing what Cane knew gave him leverage and he wouldn't hesitate to use it. He'd learned a long time ago that you had to have as much dirt on as many people as possible and then you could use it to get exactly what you wanted.

Dr. Hutchinson quickly changed the subject. "I haven't seen you in a while. What can I do for you? I know you called and left a message, but you didn't say what it was about."

"I need to know exactly what you have on Jim Rankin. He was a probable heart attack victim a little while back."

"Hold on a second," Dr. Hutchinson said. "I have dinner on and I have to make sure it doesn't overcook. Are you hungry?"

"No."

Hutchinson walked over to two large Bunsen burners, one of which had a large beaker over it while the other had a smaller one. Both beakers were over an open flame. Cane noted that there was a box of spaghetti on the counter and a corpse on a table just ten feet away in the middle of the room.

He looked back at Dr. Hutchinson and said, "What are you doing? Are you cooking dinner?"

"Yes, I am," Hutchinson said. "In one beaker spaghetti is boiling while in the other one spaghetti sauce is simmering. If you boil the spaghetti for six minutes and twelve seconds you get the most perfect *al dente* noodles imaginable. Then you simmer the sauce at low heat for exactly five minutes and twenty-one seconds and you have the perfect sauce and, in turn, you have the perfect meal. It took me an entire year to get my times precisely correct. Do you want to try some when it's done?"

Cane looked at Dr. Hutchinson and then down at the spaghetti boiling, and thought, *Great, so this is what taxpayer money is going for: the perfect spaghetti meal.* He looked at the cadaver across the room and felt a little queasy. "No, thanks. I'm not hungry."

"Suit yourself. You don't know what you're missing."

Cane shook his head again. "Now, about Jim Rankin?"

"Oh yeah, I remember him. It looks like a heart attack to me. No way to tell, though, until I get the toxicology report. But it looks like there's nothing unusual about him."

"One of the paramedics said there might have been a faint heartbeat on the way to the hospital. What do you think?"

"There could have been," Hutchinson said. "It's not that uncommon. All I know is that he was as dead as a doornail when he got here. If you have any questions about his medical care, take it up with the emergency room doctors."

Cane, feeling a little desperate and looking for an angle, said, "Why so quick on the cremation?"

"The next of kin identified the body and approved the cremation. I had already run all the tests I had to, so I sent the body over to the funeral home and they cremated right away. Legally they only have to wait twenty four hours in this state after someone is pronounced dead. Why wait? Do you expect us to stack the bodies up everywhere around here? Or do you expect the funeral home to stack the bodies up in the basement until they get around to it? If I have the chance to get rid of a stiff, I do. Do you have any more questions?"

"No, I guess that's it."

"Good, because in exactly one minute and six seconds I have to strain my spaghetti." Hutchinson pulled out a tennis racket. Cane gave him an odd look.

"What? If you strain your spaghetti with a tennis racket, it'll taste better," Hutchinson said. "If you strain it with a plastic colander, the spaghetti ends up having a slight plastic taste to it. If you strain it with metal, you can get an oxidation taste. Besides, since the noodles are slightly *al dente* and are a little sticky, they don't stick to a tennis racket like they would a metal colander. It's the only logical choice. You know, you really ought to stick around and try some."

"No, I don't think so." *Hutchinson is cooking spaghetti in a beaker next to a dead body and he's worried about how his noodles will taste if he uses a metal colander to drain them. Go figure.* Cane asked, "How long on the report?"

"I should have the results in a day or two."

"I'll be in touch. Thanks for the information." As Cane was heading out, he glanced back at the doctor and saw him looking at his watch and holding the tennis racket, making sure his timing for the noodles was just right. Cane just stared, thinking, *I knew Hutchinson was weird, but I didn't know he was that weird.*

By this time it was getting late and it was time for Cane to go back to the police station and pick up the rap sheets. When he arrived, he approached Crosby again at the front desk and said, "Hey, Crosby. Did Detective Munson leave a package for me up here?"

"Hey Cane, you dirt bag. What've you got going? Have you been hiding in the bushes looking through people's windows lately or are you just trying to cheat some little old lady out of her husband's insurance policy?"

Cane laughed and replied, "No. I'm trying to fix speeding tickets for money. Do you know anyone else who might do that?"

Crosby gave Cane a dirty look at first, then laughed. "That was a good one, you slimy parasite. Here's your package. What, did you get a rap sheet on everyone in the city? That thing is huge." He handed Cane an overstuffed file.

"Wow, I didn't think it would be this full," Cane said. "This is going to be interesting. Thanks and see you later." Crosby nodded as Cane left.

It had been a long day so he decided to go home and start fresh tomorrow. At home, he threw the file on the table and walked over to the refrigerator; the only two things in the refrigerator were an expired half-gallon of lactose-free milk and some rotten lunchmeat. He threw out both items, found some crackers in the cupboard and started eating them. He walked over to his aquarium on the other side of the room, which contained four pet mice. He picked up one of the mice and started hand-feeding it a piece of cracker.

"How is my little guy today? Is Socrates hungry? Is he? You're lucky you didn't have to deal with all the bad people I did today. But it's okay. I'll get to the bottom of things." He made a playful face as if at a baby. "Oh, my little fella is hungry. The bad people I'm dealing with are not nice. I smell a rat in the bunch. Oh, did I scare you? I didn't mean to say the word 'rat.' It's okay. You go back and play with your friends and don't worry about a thing."

He put Socrates back in his aquarium, sat down at the table and continued eating crackers. He picked up the file Detective Munson had made for him earlier and began to finger through it.

Cane noted that Munson had done his usual thorough job, including rap sheets, police reports, driving records and credit reports on all the suspects. *Boy, Munson sure does a great job for just a lunch,* Cane thought. *I'll have to give him something special one day like a gift certificate or something. On second thought, I'd better not; then he'll expect it all the time.*

That train of thought was broken as he saw Seth's file sitting right on top. Going through it thoroughly, he realized that Seth's record was clean except for one bar fight during college. No one had been hurt and the charges had been dropped. He also noticed that his driving record was clean except that he had two speeding tickets over the last seven years.

He looked at Bridget's file next and saw that she had two outstanding parking tickets that weren't paid. There was also one assault charge from several years back. She and another woman had fought over a man, exchanging blows and scratching each other up a bit. Again the charges were dropped. Cane had nothing so far; both Seth and Bridget were clean.

Bridget's credit was terrible, though. She was in deep financial trouble with four credit cards maxed out, totaling eighty thousand dollars. She was also two months behind on her house payment. Cane wondered, *What does that woman do with all her money? She took Jim Rankin to the cleaners and then blew through eighty thousand on top of it. Wow.*

He looked at the file on Brian and wasn't surprised one bit that Brian was squeaky clean. He didn't even have a parking ticket within the last seven years. His credit was good, and he owed less than two thousand dollars on one credit card. Cane had prided himself on knowing people and figured Brian was just a normal guy. Cane thought, *I knew Brian was going to be clean, but he's almost too clean. Few people are that much of a model citizen. I sure hope he doesn't have any skeletons in his closet. He seems like a nice guy and I'd hate to have to squeeze him. But I will if it comes to it. No one is above suspicion, even him.*

Now came Curt's file. It was no surprise to Cane that it had plenty in it. Curt had two assault and battery charges against him for fighting, the first instance at a bar and the second in a grocery store, of all places. The bar fight had taken place on a Saturday night when Curt had gotten in an argument over a woman. Curt and the other man beat each other up badly and he ended up pleading guilty to disturbing the peace. He received a fine and was released.

The grocery store fight was different. Apparently Curt was waiting for a parking spot and another person pulled in and took Curt's spot. When the person got out of the car, Curt and he got into a verbal confrontation, escalating into a fight with Curt throwing the first punch, according to witnesses. Cane shook his head. *What an idiot, all over a stupid parking spot.* He also saw that Curt didn't have much of a credit history, not even a credit card to speak of.

Now Cane picked up Rachelle's file, surprised at how large it was. When Cane opened it, he saw that at the age of fifteen, Rachelle had been arrested for shoplifting and got off with probation. At seventeen she was arrested for possession of marijuana, to which she pled guilty, and was also given probation. At eighteen she was arrested for prostitution, given a two hundred and fifty dollar fine and let go. At nineteen, she was arrested for minor in possession, fined two hundred and fifty dollars and let go. At twenty-one, she was arrested for check fraud; the charges were dropped. At twenty-three, she was arrested for receiving stolen goods; the charges were dropped. At twenty-four, driving under the influence of alcohol; a five hundred dollar fine and probation. At twenty-seven, assault and battery; settled out of court and the charges dropped. At twenty-eight, possession of a controlled substance. Charges dropped.

Cane set the papers down a moment and thought. *Now she's thirty-three and she's been clean for almost five years. I hope she's changed her ways, but I doubt it. For all of those charges to be dropped she must either be a master of manipulation or know someone high up in the police department. Maybe both.*

Cane looked at her driving record: it was absolutely atrocious. Six tickets over the last seven years and seven points on her record presently. He examined her credit report and realized she was nearly one hundred thousand dollars in debt with no way to pay it back except with the money from Jim's legacy and his insurance policy.

Cane frowned as he ruminated on the situation. *People like Rachelle are always going to have money troubles. No matter how much she gets, she'll always spend more than she has. She just doesn't know how to manage money. Even if she gets the five million dollar payout, she'll still end up broke one day. Look at how many people end up broke because they can't manage their money — even forty-million-dollar lottery winners or athletes that make over a hundred million end up bankrupt. Those people should be able to live the rest of their lives comfortably, but since they live extravagantly, they blow everything. If I had that kind of money, I'd make it last. I wouldn't be like Rachelle and always be spending money on ridiculous things. I'd never rack up debt like she did.*

Cane's mind turned to the practical aspects of the case. *Because Rachelle has such a shady past, there has to be some type of fraud or collusion involved with the insurance policy. There just has to be, but how? Jim died of a heart attack and Rachelle had nothing to do with it, or so it seems.*

He continued to struggle with the case the rest of the night. He figured he'd now have to focus on Rachelle because, being the sole beneficiary, she was the likely one to be dirty. Her past also made him suspicious. He went to sleep that night with anxiety and concern; his last coherent thought was, *I just have to prove fraud, or my company will be out five million dollars.*

CHAPTER 6

The next day Cane figured he'd spend most of his day watching Rachelle. He thought it might be difficult to uncover anything about her because she'd be lying low, counting on her big payout soon. Cane sat outside her place most of the day, and it was uneventful. Her blinds had been down all day except where the bedroom was. Cane wasn't even sure she was there.

In the early evening Curt drove up in front of Rachelle's apartment, got out of his car and walked up to the door and rang the buzzer. A moment later the buzzer rang to let Curt in.

A couple minutes later, Curt walked into the bedroom and Rachelle followed. Cane turned on his surveillance equipment; he knew it probably wouldn't be able to pick up a conversation inside the building, but it was worth a try.

Cane peered through his binoculars and saw Curt kiss Rachelle and push her onto the bed. She immediately pushed him away and then stood up, saying something with angry gestures. They argued for a minute and Curt left the room. A moment later, he walked out of the apartment and got in his car.

Cane guessed Rachelle would probably stay in for the rest of the night, so he decided to follow Curt. After a fifteen-minute drive, Curt ended up at an apartment building on the other side of town. Curt got out of his car and walked up to the building and rang the buzzer. A few seconds later the buzzer went off and he went in.

Fifteen minutes later, he came out with a woman who looked about twenty-three. She was about five feet six inches tall and skinny as a rail, with hair dyed purple and pink. She wore tight jeans, a black leather biker jacket and a spiked collar.

They got into Curt's car and drove about fifteen minutes to a bar in the next town called The Purple Parrot. When they began to converse in the parking lot, Cane quickly pulled out of sight and got out his surveillance equipment.

He put his earphone in just in time to hear Curt say, "Come on, babe. You know I can't stand Rachelle. You know I love you. Once I get my hands on that five million I'll drop her like a hot potato." He kissed her long and heavily as he hugged her and pressed up against her young body. "You know what we talked about. I promise once we get that money we'll get you in the recording studio and you'll make your first CD. It'll sell millions and we'll be rich and famous. Just think: we'll have to fight off fans wherever we go."

The young woman said, "Are you sure I have talent?"

"Yes, you have talent. You just need to believe in yourself and see what happens. Now go in there and knock them dead during open mic."

They kissed again and walked into the bar.

Now why would Curt be with a young punked-out girl who wasn't even half as pretty as Rachelle? Cane wondered. Then he remembered Rachelle's record and what kind of person she was. She was a user and Curt knew it. Besides, Cane knew that no matter how beautiful people are on the outside, if they are not nice on the inside they're hard to stay with.

A couple of minutes later, Cane entered the bar unobserved and sat down in the back. There were about a hundred and fifty people in the bar with more coming in, so he felt confident he would remain unnoticed. He saw that the stage was some distance away and had a fenced cage around it; that was unusual. He didn't see the girl or Curt anywhere in the bar.

About five minutes later, an announcer went onstage and said, "Welcome to the most popular part of our week: Open Mic Night." The people in the bar all clapped and cheered. The announcer continued, "Our first contestant comes all the way from Buffalo, New York. Give a warm welcome to comedian, Sam Jam!" The crowd groaned a little and just sat there.

Taking the mic, Sam Jam started with, "What do you call onions and beans? Tear gas." There were a few boos from the crowd. "What do you call a video of pedestrians?

Footage." The crowd booed more. Sam Jam continued with, "What did God say to the first man on the moon? Kneel, Armstrong." The booing was getting even louder. Sam Jam had to raise his voice to be heard over the crowd as he said, "What award did the inventor of the doorknocker receive? The no-bell prize."

Now the heckling started. "Get off the stage, you bum!" "Why don't you get a real job? You stink!" Someone threw an empty plastic beer bottle at the stage and it ricocheted off the protective fence and fell to the ground. Another man threw a plastic bottle partially full of beer, and it hit the fence and splashed on the comedian.

Cane realized that the stage was fenced to protect the performers. There was another shout of, "Get off the stage!" as more people started throwing empty beer bottles at the fence. The comedian tried to finish his set but the crowd would have none of it. They booed repeatedly until he said a few words of profanity back at the crowd and walked off the stage.

The announcer came back onstage and the crowd began to simmer down. The announcer said, "Sam Jam's jokes were sponsored by Doritos because they were both cheesy and corny." The crowd moaned and the announcer immediately went on, "I want to remind you: throwing things is not allowed while the announcer is on stage. If you do, you will be removed by a few of our less-than-friendly bouncers. Do not throw anything when I'm on stage. Our next act is becoming a regular here at The Purple Parrot. Let's give a hearty welcome to Angel Bradburn, our home-town girl."

One person yelled, "Oh no, not again."

Another person yelled, "Get her out of here."

Yet a third person yelled, "Why do you let her come back?"

Out walked Angel with Curt, who was holding what looked like a CD player. He pressed a button on the machine and set it on a stool right next to another microphone. Background music began to play as Angel began to dance awkwardly. Cane could not believe how bad she was.

She began to sing a song that he'd never heard before. The background music was terrible, which didn't help Angel's performance. Her vocals were excruciating. Someone yelled, "You stink," and threw a plastic bottle at the fence.

Someone else yelled, "Stop singing and never come back!"

Curt protectively stepped in front of Angel and yelled angrily, "Don't you know talent when you see it? You son of a—"

Before he could finish, six or seven bottles came flying up towards the stage with beer in them. They crashed up against the protective fence with a thud, splashing Curt and soaking him with beer.

One person yelled, "Get off the stage before we run out of bottles."

Curt shouted back, "I'll get you!" and lunged at the fence in a rage and rattling it as more bottles came flying up at him. He backed off, grabbed his compact disc player in one hand and Angel's hand in the other, and said, "Come on, let's get out of here." They ran until they were safely backstage.

Cane was appalled. *My Lord. That was one of the worst, most painful things I've seen in a long time. Why would she put herself through that type of punishment to become a singer? She must really want it bad.* He chuckled, thinking, *at least they sell a lot of beer here, because half of it gets thrown at the performers.* Cane rose from his seat, went out to his car and waited.

Curt and Angel soon came out; as they neared their car, Cane could now hear them with his surveillance device. Angel began to cry, saying, "I told you I wasn't any good. I'm terrible."

"Come on, babe, you were terrific. Those people just don't know talent when they see it."

Cane couldn't believe his ears. *How could Curt tell her that? Maybe that old saying is true: love is blind. No, it can't be that blind. He must be deaf; I don't care how much he loves her, he couldn't have possibly thought her performance was good. What is his deal? Why is he with her?*

"Don't worry, babe. All of these people who were mean to you will be sorry when you won't even look at them, when you're on stage with fifty thousand people screaming your name. All we have to do is get that money and you'll be doing concerts all over the country. You just wait and see. You're going to be a star."

"Do you promise, Curt?"

"I promise."

Cane thought, *That's a promise that will never be kept.*

Curt continued, "Look at the bright side. You smell just like Budweiser and that's my favorite beer." They both laughed a little; then Curt kissed Angel. "Yeah. A Budweiser would taste great about now."

"Oh Curt, I love you," said Angel. They kissed again and got into Curt's car. Cane followed them back to Angel's apartment; he figured they were in for the night, so he drove back home.

As he got ready for bed, he couldn't stop thinking about the case. It was one of the weirdest cases he'd ever been on; he couldn't believe that almost every single person involved was cheating on another person and in love with someone else.

If this keeps up I'll have to hire an assistant to keep track of everyone. I wonder what'll happen next? Is Brian going to have two or three women as well? He collected his thoughts and remembered that no matter how deceitful everyone was to one another, his company would still have to pay out unless he could prove fraud or misrepresentation.

All of a sudden Cane didn't feel so well, knowing that he really didn't have a case.

Soon he would be forced to come up with a viable reason to ask for an extension and for more time to pursue leads. He knew he had up to ninety days to solve the case, but would need a viable reason to make it last more than thirty days. Cane also knew he had to file for an extension well in advance and that his time would soon be running short. He felt a little down. If he didn't come up with something soon, his company would be paying out one of the largest policies in its history.

He did the one thing that always calmed him down: he picked up his mice and played with them. Replacing the animals after a few minutes, he laid down and went to sleep still going over the case in his head, searching for a clue.

$ $ $

Cane woke the next morning and quickly got ready and rushed off. He had to get some dirt on Rachelle, and he had to get it fast. He was a master at stirring things up and putting pressure on people; then he would sit back, wait for them to make a mistake and crack, and pounce on them like a wildcat on its prey. He knew exactly what buttons to push to make people's blood boil with rage, and he didn't care about his effect on their lives as long as he solved the case.

The first thing he did was head over to Rachelle's house with a pair of rubber gloves. He knew the south side of the city had trash pickup that day, so he started going through her trash that was set out at the curb. As her apartment building had afternoon pick-up, he had plenty of time to let Rachelle see him out there. Cane really didn't expect to find anything useful. He just wanted Rachelle or Curt to do or say something stupid so he could use it against them.

Cane made sure to be very loud as he rummaged through the garbage; he even knocked over the cans a couple of times just to be sure of being noticed. Sure enough, Rachelle came outside after seeing Cane digging around out front with Curt by her side.

When Rachelle approached Cane, she said, "What are you doing?"

In a sarcastic tone Cane said, "What does it look like I'm doing? I'm going through your garbage. You'd be surprised what you can find out about people from what they throw out."

Curt, ever the hothead, got right in Cane's face and said, "Yeah, well, that's harassment."

"Actually it's not harassment, because I'm not a cop. And, if you have nothing to hide, then what do you care?"

Curt looked like he was going to do something stupid. Rachelle quickly jumped in, touched Curt's arm and said softly, "We don't want to hinder Mr. Cane in any way." She shot Curt a covert wink and said, "Curt, can you excuse us for a moment?" He backed off, walked away a bit and left Cane alone with Rachelle.

She sidled up to Cane, laid her hand seductively on his arm and began, "Mr. Cane, I realize you're just a man trying to do his job. If there's any way I can help you or if there is anything I can do for you, let me know. A man like you must have certain needs." Cane stopped rummaging through the trash, looked up at Rachelle and realized she was attempting to use her beauty to entice him, as she had probably done to many men before.

It was crystal clear to Cane now how Rachelle had gotten out of trouble with the law all those years. She used her seductive ways to manipulate people into doing exactly what she wanted, including dropping any charges against her.

Rachelle was a very beautiful woman, so Cane had to summon his strength, determination and motivation to resist her advances and replied, "As a matter of fact, you could do something for me; you could answer a few questions. How did Jim Rankin ever get involved with you? I know you were a nightclub dancer from the check I ran on you, and I know how many times you were arrested and for what. You always seem to get out of whatever scrape you're in. I just want to know how and why Jim Rankin picked you to ask to marry him and to set up a five million dollar policy with you as the sole beneficiary. On top of that, tell me what the odds are for him to die a month later. I find that a little too coincidental. If you really want to do something for me, explain how something like this could happen." Cane fixed a wide-eyed stare on Rachelle, waiting for a reaction.

Rachelle simply said, "Jim and I were in love. And besides, I didn't even know he took out the policy."

"Oh really? Then how come your signature is on the policy?"

"Jim had me sign all sorts of papers. I hardly ever knew what I was signing."

"I see. So you're saying that you had no idea you were the beneficiary of a five million dollar policy until the day at the attorney's office when you were told?"

"Yes, that's right."

"Because of your past history, I have a hard time believing a word you say. I'm going to prove fraud in this case."

Just then Curt walked up and said, "I heard exactly what you said. You're speaking to a lady and don't you forget it." Seeing Cane smirk, he stepped closer to Cane and said, "You think it's funny about Rachelle being a lady? How about I break your neck right now and then you won't have to worry about it?"

Rachelle jumped in between them and said, "Don't make a mistake, Curt. He has nothing on us. His company is going to be paying us soon, and I'm going to ask that Mr. Cane hand deliver the check personally to us."

That made Cane furious; he hated losing a case more than almost anything. "We'll see about that! I've got exactly what I came for," he cried, and grabbed a soiled phone bill from the garbage, putting it in a plastic baggie and sealing it. After getting back to his car, he drove away, circled the block out of sight and pulled up around the corner. He yanked out his surveillance equipment to try to catch the tail end of Curt and Rachelle's reaction to what he said.

They thought he was long gone. Cane heard Curt saying, "You should've let me rough him up right there. He would've thought twice about messing with us and investigating this case."

"No," said Rachelle, "that probably would have been what he wanted. Cane is a crafty little weasel. He'd love for us to do something stupid so he could delay paying us out. Besides, he would have filed charges against you and there would've been an investigation. I said before, you let me do the thinking and just do what I tell you, got it?"

Curt wasn't about to disagree with Rachelle with so much money on the line and with his other girlfriend's future depending on the settlement, so he bit his lip and kept quiet.

Rachelle continued, "Cane knows his time is running out and that's why he's trying to provoke us into doing something stupid. I'm not going to let a little twit like him outsmart me. I have a friend down at the vice squad in the third precinct who owes me a big favor. I have dirt on him and he'll help me out if I ask. The thing we need to do is find out everything we can about Cane. If you want to control somebody, you have to get information so you can take them down. Everyone has their weaknesses, and Cane must have a few skeletons in his closet. We just have to find them. Take me over to the third precinct right now and let me work my magic."

When they drove off, Cane tried to follow them, but lost them in traffic, so he headed for the third precinct to try to catch up with them again. He knew he didn't have strong connections over at the third precinct, so he decided to just wait outside. On the way there, he considered, *If Rachelle thinks she can outsmart me, she has another thing coming. As long as I can keep listening to her conversations I can always be one step ahead of her. If she thinks she has connections at the police department, she has no idea how many cops I know. I still have to be careful though; with her past there's no telling what she might do. And that hothead Curt could get dangerous. They may keep their cool well enough to get the payout, but if I prove fraud, I'm really going to have to watch it.*

When he arrived at the police station, Rachelle and Curt were already inside. Rachelle asked to see Lieutenant O'Brien. When Lieutenant O'Brien arrived he didn't look happy at all to see her

Rachelle said, "I need to see you in your office right away."

O'Brien sighed and replied, "Of course. Follow me."

Rachelle told Curt to wait outside the office and Curt agreed.

When they got into O'Brien's office, Rachelle said, "How are your wife and kids?"

O'Brien said, "All right, Rachelle. You know what we did was wrong. I love my wife so back off."

"Relax," Rachelle said. "Have I not kept my end of it quiet?"

"What do you want? I'm sure you wouldn't be here unless you wanted something."

"Do you know a weird insurance investigator by the name of Wendell Cane?" said Rachelle.

"Sure I do. Everyone knows him. What's up?"

"I need you to tell me everything you know about him."

O'Brien replied, "There isn't really much to tell about him. I know he's kind of a weirdo. He has pet rats or something and plays with them, I guess. I know he works for Philadelphia Mutual and is actually one of the best insurance investigators in the state. It's not easy to get anything past him, from what I've heard. He's unraveled some of the trickiest cases of fraud you could imagine."

Rachelle sighed and said, "Is he married or does he have any kids? What do you know about him?"

"Are you joking?" O'Brien said. "Wendell Cane? His clothes don't even match. Do you think he'd have a wife? He's married to his job and takes it seriously."

She mumbled under her breath, "Well, blackmail is out."

"I'm sorry, I didn't hear you. What did you say?"

"Oh, nothing. Is there anything else I should know?"

"The word is he's a strict, straightforward, honest guy, so if I were you I wouldn't get any funny ideas. Why do you need to know so much about him, or should I know better than to ask?"

Rachelle said quickly, "No reason. I just wanted to know. Thanks for the information." O'Brien didn't really want anything to do with Rachelle so he didn't question her any further.

As Rachelle was leaving, O'Brien said, "Now I've done you your favor. If you get in trouble, I don't want you calling me. You're on your own."

Rachelle said, "Don't worry. Our secret is safe," and left.

On the way back to the car, she told Curt what she had learned about Cane. "He's going to be a tough one to crack. He's just such a dork. We don't have any leverage to squeeze him. Come on, let's go to my house and figure out how to get this geek."

Rather than follow them back to her apartment, Cane decided to go to the coroner's office to get the final autopsy report.

$ $ $

On arriving at the county morgue, Cane approached the receptionist and said, "May I see Dr. Hutchinson? I'm hoping the autopsy is in on Rankin."

The receptionist picked up the phone, dialed an extension and said, "Cane is here for the report on Rankin. Should I send him back? All right." She hung up and told Cane, "You can go on back; it's not like you need anyone to escort you. You know the way and besides, we never had anyone walk off with a stiff before. Get it? Walk off with a stiff?" She laughed a little and added, "He's waiting for you."

As Cane approached, Dr. Hutchinson called, "Cane! Hurry! You're just in time."

Cane thought, *Maybe Hutchinson has some news I can use about Jim Rankin!* Cane's stomach fluttered with nerves as he replied, "Just in time for what?"

"Just in time for cheesy franks."

Cane looked at the doctor in growing revulsion.

Hutchinson explained, "What you do is take a Ball Park frank and wrap bacon around it. Then you put a slit in the end and stuff cheese in it. After that you broil them in the toaster oven for six minutes and forty-two seconds. They turn out perfect."

"You have a toaster oven right here in the morgue?"

"Yeah, why not?" Dr Hutchinson said. "I use it when I want to cook something special. The heat from the oven kills all the germs. I don't see anything wrong with it. Cheesy franks are the perfect meal. I have six of them right here. Do you want to try one?"

Cane's stomach turned a little. "No thanks, I already ate."

Hutchinson said, "To each his own. You don't know what you're missing."

"What about the autopsy report on Rankin?"

"You have to excuse me. I have to eat while we talk. These cheesy franks have to be eaten no more than seven minutes and sixteen seconds after they come out of the oven or the cheese will begin to harden again. The window of opportunity for a perfect frank will be gone after that."

"By all means, eat. I just want to know about the autopsy."

Hutchinson took a bite of his hot dog and said in a muffled voice, "Yeah, I prepared that report just a couple of hours ago. As a matter of fact, I have it right here." Cane looked up and noticed that there was a dead body just three feet away, covered up on the table next to them. Cane gulped with a dry throat as he peered at the doctor, waiting for some information.

The doctor paused to swallow his food as Cane said, "Well? What does it say?"

Hutchinson had a cheesy frank in one hand and opened the folder with his other as he took another bite of his hot dog. "Let's see. He had no prescription drugs or illegal substances in the bloodstream, not even so much as a Motrin. This guy was as clean as a whistle. He had an enlarged coronary artery and blockage in his left ventricle. He died of a heart attack."

Cane stared. "Are you sure? I can't believe it."

Hutchinson took another bite of his cheesy frank and said, "I'm absolutely sure. It's more than obvious."

Cane took a deep breath in disappointment and said, "All right. Thanks."

"Are you sure you don't want to try these? They're smoking good. Get it? Smoking good? You got about two more minutes before they lose their perfection." The investigator shook his head and walked out the door.

Cane was rarely wrong when it came to cases and judging people, but apparently he was wrong this time. He had been sure there was some type of fraud or foul play in this case until he saw the autopsy report. Worse, now his company was going to have to pay out one of the biggest policies ever and there was nothing he could do about it.

He was feeling depressed, with no leads or hope of proving the wrongdoing he so strongly suspected. He went home to play with his mice as he usually did to forget his problems.

CHAPTER 7

The next morning, Cane went to work as usual, spent a half hour going over the case in his office, and decided to check out Rachelle's phone bill. He pulled the soiled bill from his desk and noticed it was from two months prior. As he looked it over, he saw that there was one number that she had called almost every day and several that appeared to be mere random calls. Cane picked up his office phone and dialed the number Rachelle had called so many times.

Someone picked up and said, "Hello."

Cane recognized the voice as Curt's and said quickly, "Is this Curt?"

"Yeah, it's Curt. Who's this?"

It wouldn't hurt to stir things up some more, Cane thought. "It's Wendell Cane. I didn't mean to bother you. I'm just checking out all the phone calls Rachelle made recently. I see she called you almost every day while she was engaged to Jim."

Curt raised his voice and said, "You little piece of crap, Cane! Who do you think you are? I ought to come over there right now and beat the living—"

Just then Rachelle grabbed the phone and said "This is harassment! If you call this phone again I'll have you brought up on charges. Got it?"

"Sorry, I was just checking who you called every day when you and Jim were engaged."

Rachelle calmly said, "You have nothing on us. You know that me calling him doesn't mean a thing. So stop harassing us and get the check ready." She hung up.

Angry at being taunted, Cane took a deep breath and focused back on the case. *She's right. Unless I can prove there was some type of fraud or misrepresentation, the calls mean nothing. But if there is fraud, those calls could be the best evidence.*

$ $ $

He spent the next half hour calling every number on the bill and came up with no leads. Just before lunch, he was interrupted by the phone ringing.

"Wendell Cane here."

"This is Detective Munson."

"Yes?"

Munson said, "You'd better get down to the station right away. An attempt was just made on Rachelle Johnson's life. How long will it take you to get down here?"

"No more than fifteen minutes."

"Good. Hurry up. You'd better get here before things blow up in our faces. There seems to be trouble brewing and we're going to get to the bottom of it."

"I'll be right over." Cane hung up the phone, feeling suddenly rejuvenated. He knew everyone involved with the case was unstable. He also knew that he was dealing with a bunch of two-timing cheaters who would probably sell out their own mothers if they had to. He'd hoped that one of them would snap under pressure and his case would be blown wide open. Maybe this was it.

When Cane arrived at the police station, he went up to Crosby. "Munson is expecting me. Can I go back?"

Crosby laughed and said, "Cane, you never cease to amaze me. I would have thought that the ugly patrol would have arrested you by now and never allowed you back in our town again."

Cane grinned and followed immediately with, "Did your wife leave you yet? I would've thought she would have asked for a divorce about fifteen minutes after she married you."

Crosby laughed and said, "At least I have a wife."

Cane groaned, "Oh, good one. Where's Munson?"

Crosby motioned to Cane to go on back; on the way, Cane felt a little hurt. Even though Crosby's and his exchanges were always harmless, the comment about not having a wife hit him where it counted. He dismissed the sadness. *Hey, I made a choice about my job a long time ago. At least my job doesn't talk back to me, and at least I'm a respected investigator in my company. I probably could have had a wife, but I never really had a girlfriend. I have no regrets about giving up so much for my job.*

Munson came up and said, "All the people involved with the case are already here in separate interrogation rooms. Rachelle Johnson and Curt Clark are giving their statements. Apparently they were walking just outside of Rachelle's apartment building when a blue late-model Chrysler mini-van swerved up onto the sidewalk, almost hitting Rachelle. From what I was told, Rachelle barely had enough time to move out of the way. Then the van sped off. No one got a license plate number or a description of the driver. Ms. Johnson is pretty upset."

"Oh, I'm sure she is," Cane said sarcastically.

Munson continued, "Brian Williams, Seth Rankin, and Bridget Bartkowski have all been questioned about their whereabouts when the incident occurred. We have everyone's statement. All three of them have solid alibis."

"I have an idea," Cane said. "Why don't we get all five of them in the same room at once and ask them some questions and stir things up a bit? When you get two women like Bridget and Rachelle together, sparks will fly and someone will do something stupid, which could lead to some clues. We can get them all riled up and turn them loose on one another."

"You're a genius, Cane. We haven't used that trick in quite a while. No wonder Philadelphia Mutual stays in business. Give me a minute, and I'll get them all ready in room four. Oh, and let me turn the air conditioning off to make it even more uncomfortable in there."

"Now you're the genius. One of them will break down for sure."

The suspects were soon brought in together by Munson's partner Detective Ramsey. Munson began by saying, "As you know, today there was an apparent attempt on Ms. Johnson's life."

Rachelle said, "What do you mean, 'apparent'? Are you insinuating anything?"

"No," Munson said. "It's just that we've had false reports filed before, and no one actually did see it happen but you two. We just want to make sure you're not corroborating each other's story."

"Yeah, right. We made the whole thing up just to divert attention away from us," Rachelle said.

Munson responded, "Let me write this down. You're saying you did make it up just to divert attention away from you?"

"You know I was just being cynical," she sneered.

Munson said, "Cynicism is something I don't like."

"Let me tell you, if the person comes back and tries something like that again, he's going to find himself in a six foot hole with dirt on top of him," Curt said.

Munson started writing on a pad of paper and said, "Really? That sounds like a threat."

"Call it what you want," Rachelle said. "I call it self-defense. And furthermore, you'll be hearing from my lawyer about a civil suit."

Munson laughed. "Don't flatter yourself. I've dealt with people like you for years. If you think you're going to try to outsmart me, good luck." He turned to Brian, Bridget and Seth. "What about you three? You have the biggest motive in the world to want Miss Johnson dead: your share of five million dollars comes to mind."

The temperature was getting noticeably warmer in the room, and Cane could tell that tempers would soon be escalating because everyone seemed to look uncomfortable. He hoped Munson would keep the pressure on.

"Are we being charged with anything?" Bridget asked. "If so, I'd like to see my lawyer."

"See, she's the one!" Curt cried. "I knew it! All she cares about is getting her grubby little hands on our money."

Munson replied, "And what is it you care about, Curt?"

Curt took a deep breath and thought a moment and said, "I care about Rachelle's safety. Now are you going to arrest these two or not?"

Seth, who was beginning to sweat, shot back, "Shut up, you loudmouth! He has nothing on us and we have ironclad alibis. Besides, we wouldn't waste our time on scum like you."

Curt stood up and started towards Seth, who stood to meet him, shouting, "Bring it on, loser."

"I'll teach you a lesson, fat boy," yelled Curt, and leaped toward Seth.

Munson and Ramsey jumped between Seth and Curt just in time. Munson yelled, "Sit down, both of you, or I'll send you off to jail together!" He grabbed Seth, his partner grabbed Curt, and they pulled them apart.

Catching his breath, Munson sat down, saying, "I'm going to forget I saw that."

"Why?" said Curt. "I just want to teach fat boy over there a little lesson that he won't forget. He'd better get used to defending himself if you're sending him to jail. He may as well start now."

"That'll be enough of that," Munson said.

Cane was inwardly pleased that everyone was riled up, including the women. *The plan is working perfectly so far.*

They're all at each other's throats. Then he noticed Brian sitting calmly, basically unconcerned by the events. That was intriguing. *Is he truly unconcerned, or does he have something to hide that I don't see?*

His trend of thought was broken by Munson saying, "Now that you've all calmed down, I want to say I smell a rat. Five million dollars is too much money to be playing around with. Did you know that attempted murder gets you a minimum of ten years in this state?"

Rachelle spoke up and said, "What about me? I'm the victim here and you're treating me like a common criminal. These people almost took my life."

"We can't even be sure it wasn't an accident, and besides, we don't have any evidence to hold them," Munson said.

"Well, are you at least going to provide me with police protection?"

"I'm sorry, Ms. Johnson," said Munson, "we can't provide you with twenty-four-hour protection. The department has had too many cutbacks lately and my chief would have my head if I even suggested it. The best we can do is send a black and white unit around every so often to make sure you're safe."

Curt said sarcastically, "Yeah, that's just another case of our tax dollars never being used for something that's needed. Don't worry, Rachelle. I'll be ready for them the next time these amateurs try this again. I'll make them sorry they ever heard our names."

"I'm warning you, Mr. Clark. Don't take the law into your own hands," said Munson.

"I have to defend myself since you and your men won't."

Munson scowled. "Don't be a hero." He turned to Seth and Bridget. "Let me remind you two that if you're involved with the attempt on her life, you'd better quit while you're ahead. If there is another attempt on her life, I'll have you both in here with shackles on. Let me remind you we have the death penalty in this state for premeditated murder. So keep your noses clean." To Cane he said, "Is there anything you want to add?"

"As a matter of fact, I would like to add something," said Cane. "I got the autopsy report yesterday and apparently Jim Rankin did die of a heart attack. There seemed to be no unusual substances in his system. I really wouldn't have believed it if I hadn't read it myself in the report. I was sure one of you bozos was involved. I still think there's something funny about this case, and I'm going to find out what it is."

Rachelle said, "Well, that must mean my check is going to be in the mail if suspicions are all you have."

"On the contrary," Cane said. "If you read the fine print in the policy, we can ask for an extension for payout if our investigation isn't complete. I'm going to ask for thirty days. That's the first extension. I can ask for up to two more if I so choose." Cane was just trying to make Curt and Rachelle mad knowing he had to have a good reason to ask for all that time. It worked because Curt blurted out, "Another thirty days. Are you kidding me?"

Cane wanted to say, "Don't worry, your little girlfriend can wait. Her singing is so pitiful all the money in the world won't help her anyway." But he held back. He knew it was pointless right now to divulge the fact that Curt was two-timing Rachelle; he wanted to save that tidbit of information for leverage until he really needed it.

Curt said, "We don't want to wait for the money any longer. I don't think I can take this bull—"

Rachelle cut Curt off. "If Mr. Cane feels he's missing something, that's his prerogative. All I have to say to you, Mr. Cane, is this: you're not missing anything. Your company is going to have to pay that money out to me, and that's a fact. You may be able to use your stall tactics for another thirty days, and that's fine. But remember one thing. If you stall any longer, I'll have my attorney sue you for unreasonably holding out on the payout and you can take that to the bank, no pun intended."

Cane just put his hands up in the air, shrugged his shoulders and said, "So be it."

Rachelle continued, "It's okay if Detective Munson doesn't want to give me protection. I'll be getting my own protection."

Munson shook his head. "I'm warning you, Ms. Johnson, not to take the law into your own hands."

"Take the law into my own hands? I do have the right to protect myself, don't I?"

"Of course you do. I just don't want to see you end up in jail for doing something stupid."

"Don't worry about me. I have a habit of doing the sensible thing."

Silence was the only response. Finally Munson said, "All right. You're all free to go."

After everyone had left but Cane, Munson and Ramsey, Cane commented, "That was brilliant how you pushed

Curt's buttons like that. You had him like a puppet on a string."

"Yeah, it's easy to get under a hothead's skin. I'll tell you right now that Seth and Bridget are definitely guilty. I've been on this job too long to not realize that. You have a real bunch of winners on your hands. Good luck with this one."

"I know they're a bunch of degenerates," Cane said. "I also know they all have something to hide. But if I don't find something soon, Philadelphia Mutual is going to be out five million, and my boss is going to hit the roof."

"Maybe they do have something to hide," said Munson, "but I just don't see you getting around this one."

"Hey, what did you think of Brian Williams just sitting there calmly the entire time?"

"I don't know about him. Either he's really clean and not in this mess, or he's smart and he's hiding something. He seems a tough one to crack."

Cane agreed. "He's a little too calm for me. Only time will tell, though. See you later." As he left, he thought about what his next move would be.

$ $ $

After Seth and Bridget left the police station, they took a ride together to discuss the situation. Bridget said, "You idiot! I told you to hire someone to get the job done and you hired an amateur. Now it's going to be impossible to take her out."

"The guy got cold feet and swerved away at the last minute. I can't help it if he lost his nerve," Seth protested as he drove.

"That's what I get for dealing with a bumbling idiot like you."

"Come on, baby. You know I love you. Don't talk to me like that. Let's go to your place and forget about all this for a little while."

"No way! I have too much to think about. It's going to be twice as hard now to get to Rachelle. And you heard that nut Cane say we have only thirty days. I'm going to have to plan this out for when she least expects it. This time I'll take care of it myself. I should've known better than to trust you in the first place. I have a friend who'll help me and there won't be any mistakes. I'm not going to let some former table dancer take from me what is rightfully mine. In the meantime, you're not going to lay as much as a finger on me until I come up with a plan to take care of Rachelle."

Seth whined, "Oh come on, baby."

"No, not one finger until we take care of Rachelle. Now take me back to my car so I can go home."

$ $ $

Meanwhile, Rachelle and Curt were having a discussion of their own. It started with Rachelle saying, "I can't believe that witch tried to kill me."

"Don't worry, I won't let it happen again."

"I'm not going to let it happen again," Rachelle said. "I'm going to buy a handgun and carry it in my purse from now on. Take me to the Exit Club where I used to work a couple of months ago. I can get a .38 caliber for a hundred and a quarter. Then I'll be safe."

Curt turned the car around and headed in the direction of the club where Rachelle used to work. "You should've let me teach fat boy a lesson," he said. "Then he'd think twice about coming after us again."

Rachelle shook her head and said, "That's why I do all the thinking for us. You wanted to get in a fight in a police station in front of a cop? How stupid can you be? It's a wonder you aren't in jail already with the way you can't control your temper and the way you act before you think."

Curt didn't say a word, partly because he was intellectually outmatched, and partly because he didn't care what Rachelle said. He just wanted to get his hands on the money she had coming. They had known each other for five years now and used each other in more ways than one.

"Hopefully I'll have that .38 by the end of the day," Rachelle said. "I don't trust Bridget one bit. In fact, the way she walks around thinking she can destroy anyone in her path, she reminds me of Godzilla. Yeah, that's a perfect name for her: Godzilla."

$ $ $

Cane had left the police station discouraged that his case was at an impasse. He had one last ray of hope: to go through Jim's apartment, looking for anything that might help prove Rachelle committed fraud. Cane was desperate, and desperation called for desperate measures.

It was getting late. Cane headed over to Jim's apartment building and knocked on the manager's door. The manager was a bald, heavyset man with what looked like a spare tire around his waist, wearing a faded and yellowed undershirt and tattered shorts that didn't match. He had a half-burned, unlit cigar in his mouth; it looked as if he had been chewing on it for a while.

Cane said, "I'm Wendell Cane, an insurance investigator, and I was wondering if I could take a look at Jim Rankin's apartment. I'm investigating a claim on his death and it would be helpful if I could look around."

The manager growled, "Can't do it. The rent is paid up for two more months by the lawyer. I can't let anyone take anything until some lady named Rachelle Johnson comes and removes all the stuff. If she doesn't take it in two months, she forfeits it. After that you can have what you want. The apartment is the same as when he died. I can't let you go in there."

Cane pulled out a fifty-dollar bill and said, "I don't want to take anything. I just want to look around."

The manager said, "I don't think you understand. It's against the law to let you in without the beneficiary's approval."

Cane pulled out another fifty-dollar bill and then looked at the manager, who hesitated and said, "Ah, I really can't let you in."

Cane pulled out another fifty and said, "That's the last of it."

"Well, I guess it wouldn't hurt if you just took a look around, as long as you don't take anything."

"I won't touch a thing," Cane said.

"You have fifteen minutes, and that's it."

Cane handed the manager one of the bills and said, "You get the other two when I'm in the apartment."

The manager grabbed the key from a pegboard next to his door and led the way to Jim's apartment. He opened the door and said, "Here you go."

Cane handed him the other two fifties.

"Thanks. Remember: fifteen minutes, and don't take anything."

"Fine." Cane shut the door and immediately started looking around. The first thing he noticed was that everything was extremely neat, clean, and well organized. He snooped around for a few minutes and found nothing unusual.

He walked over to the answering machine and pushed the playback button. There was one message from the library about an overdue book, and another about picking up dry cleaning. He removed the answering machine tape and put it in his pocket, then headed into the bedroom, feeling discouraged.

There was a cedar box on Jim's dresser. Leafing through the papers in it, he thought, *What a waste of time.* At the bottom of the stack was a paper that was completely folded up. It was Jim's last credit card statement. Cane read it through and a light came on in his head. *Yes, finally. Now I see. I knew something wasn't right about this case. Maybe Rachelle had something to do with Jim's death after all. Everything seems to be falling in place.* He folded up the credit card bill and stuck it in his pocket.

On the kitchen table, he found Jim's bank statement from the month before he died, and after reading it carefully, he pocketed that as well There was nothing else useful to be found, and he knew his time allotted by the manager was coming to an end, so he walked out and went back to the manager's apartment. "I'm done. I didn't find anything unusual," Cane said. The manager nodded as Cane left.

In his car he thought, *Yes. Now I can get to the bottom of this. There is a ray of hope after all.* He drove home with a new feeling of purpose.

CHAPTER 8

Cane woke up the next morning still feeling invigorated and full of hope. The best thing to do now was try to stir things up with Bridget as he'd done with Rachelle. Today was her trash day, so he drove over to her house, got his rubber gloves on, and started digging through her garbage. Once again, he was deliberately loud so Bridget would know he was there.

A few minutes later, Bridget came out of the house and was apparently on her way to work when she noticed him out front. He had two garbage bags full of trash laid out by the curb; when he saw Bridget coming, he picked up his camera and pretended to photograph her trash.

Bridget walked up and asked, "What in the world do you think you're doing?"

"I'm just doing my job: gathering evidence."

"You're doing your job by scattering my trash all over the street? This is harassment. That's what it is. I guarantee you'll be hearing from my lawyer."

Cane said, "I've been doing this job for twenty years and I know what I can do and what I can't. The fact that you placed your garbage in the street off your property means that I can go through it at will. I don't play by the same rules as the police do."

"Well, we'll see about that. You are one of the most appallingly repulsive people I've ever met. It's disgusting and ridiculous that you would even *consider* digging through someone's trash, let alone doing it! You're one of the most vile people in the world."

Wanting to get under her skin, he replied, "Really? I'm surprised you feel that way because most women find me very attractive. You know, I'm quite a ladies' man."

That wasn't the negative reaction Bridget was hoping for so she just stood there festering. Cane continued, "You think I'm unusual? I find it extremely unusual for a woman to marry a good decent man and then cheat on him with two different men in one week. Do you think that's normal? Apparently you must, because you did it." Bridget looked as if she was ready to strike Cane but held back.

He went on: "I also find it unusual that a man takes out a five million dollar insurance policy on himself and names a table dancer that he barely knows as a beneficiary. I find it unusual that he dies a month later. I find it even more unusual that you're next in line to get a portion of the money if anything happens to Rachelle and then suddenly there's an attempt on her life. In fact, I find that to be too much of a coincidence for me to believe. You see, this is no longer about the settlement. It's personal, and I'm sure there'll be an attempted murder charge somewhere down the line. So if you want to talk about me being unusual, I can talk all day about unusual things."

As if the conversation was over, he stooped and began digging through the trash again, calmly humming a favorite song.

"Who do you think you are, talking to me like that?" Bridget demanded. "For your information, Jim was a freaky little geek who could never do anything for himself. You don't know what it was like for me. I needed someone to help me cope with life. And as far as attempted murder, you have nothing on me and you know it. I have a rock solid alibi and wouldn't waste my time on that witch anyway. If I had been the one to make an attempt on her life, she wouldn't be walking around now. So get out of here and leave me alone."

Cane kept humming and digging through the trash, hoping she might become angry enough to say something she didn't intend, or do something stupid and incriminating.

Bridget could control herself no longer; she kicked the garbage can as hard as she could. It went flying and almost hit Cane's leg. Raging toward her car, she shouted, "I'll take care of you. Just wait and see." She backed out in her car recklessly and sped away with tires squealing.

Cane smirked. *You're a genius. You got exactly what you wanted out of that. She's so mad she's bound to make a mistake. When you get through with her, you'll have her acting like a puppet on a string.*

$ $ $

Next, Cane staked out Rachelle's apartment for about an hour; finally, she and Curt walked out, cautiously got into Curt's car, and drove off. Cane followed at a distance to avoid being seen. Eventually, in one of the least desirable parts of town, they pulled up in front of the Exit Club where Rachelle had worked, easing into an alley behind the building. After five minutes, another car pulled up behind them. The driver got out and so did Rachelle and Curt. Cane focused his surveillance device and binoculars on Rachelle.

The driver looked about twenty-five years old, with baggy jeans that sagged below his waist and a New York Yankees baseball cap turned backward, beneath which he had shaved his head to stubble. He asked the couple, "Did you come alone?"

Curt said, "Of course we came alone."

"Did you bring the money?"

"Yeah, we have the money. Did you bring the pieces?"

The driver pulled out two handguns and said, "that'll be three hundred."

"You said two fifty," countered Rachelle.

"The price just went up. With inflation what do you expect?"

"Inflation?" said Curt. "It's been just one day."

The young man said, "My cost goes up, your cost goes up. You wanted the pieces and I got them. If you want them, it's three hundred."

Rachelle turned to Curt and said, "We want them. Just pay him." Curt pulled a roll of cash out of his pocket and counted out three hundred dollars. The man took the money, counted it again and handed over the guns.

"If you need anything else, you know where to find me."

"Trust me," Curt said. "We won't need any more. We got these strictly for protection."

"If you get caught with those you better not tell where you got them or you'll be in a world of trouble. You don't want me and my boys coming down on you."

Rachelle said, "Don't worry about us. We would never turn you in."

"Good. It's been a pleasure doing business with you." The man jumped back into the car and drove off.

Pocketing the rest of his money, Curt said, "Let's see that skanky little witch try something now. I'll put a cap in her without thinking twice."

"Calm down, superman," Rachelle said. "Be smart for once in your life. We have five million coming to us. Don't do anything to jeopardize that."

Cane thought he really couldn't blame Rachelle for wanting a gun. After all, there had been an attempt on her life and the police were no help. She could've hired a bodyguard to protect herself, but that would have been very expensive and she didn't have that kind of money yet.

I should be careful how far I push Rachelle and Curt, Cane reminded himself. *There's no telling how much Curt will take before he snaps, and now that he has a gun, he could be dangerous. No need to make this case any harder than it has to be.*

Another important idea came to him. *The good thing about their carrying handguns is that, if it comes to it, I could have them arrested for carrying concealed weapons. Then I'd have grounds to ask for another extension on the basis of their alleged criminal activity.*

He followed Rachelle and Curt back to her apartment at a safe distance. After a half hour with no activity, he found himself thinking, *Why aren't those people calling me back about the charges on Jim's card? Those charges have to be the answer; they just have to.*

Cane waited another half hour and decided to go home. On the way, he pondered why he'd become an insurance investigator in the first place, and why he'd stayed one for so long. He knew the answer: he loved the thrill of the chase. He loved to hunt down information and prove people wrong while saving his company money.

A smile of satisfaction came to his face. Even if he lost this case, there would be others. He'd have plenty of opportunities to stir up people's lives and watch them squirm. He went to sleep that night feeling confident that the case would resolve in his favor.

$ $ $

The next day was trash day for Brian, and Cane planned to try the same trick on him. *Brian's still a suspect in the attempted murder of Rachelle,* Cane thought. *Even though he hasn't done anything to warrant concern, he's still not above suspicion.*

He arrived at Brian's place and began going through the trash as he had with Rachelle and Bridget. Cane almost laughed at what he saw: *Brian has the neatest garbage I've ever seen. Even inside the garbage bags it has some kind of order. The papers are all together in a plastic grocery bag and the food products are all in another bag. I mean, who organiz-es their trash? This is going to be easy to go through.* After about twenty minutes of making noise and digging around, he heard Brian finally come out.

"What are you doing?"

"Hello, Mr. Williams. I'm looking for evidence."

Brian laughed. "You've got to be kidding me. I've heard of people doing stuff like this before, but I never thought people actually would stoop that low. Are you out of clues or just trying to make me mad? You must be really desper-ate for evidence. Is your case not going very well, Mr. Cane?"

"On the contrary, things are moving right along."

"Well, if they are, why are you digging in my garbage? Forget it. I shouldn't even ask."

"Why does it make you mad that I'm digging in your garbage?"

Brian laughed again. "It doesn't. You can come over here every week and dig in my garbage if it makes you feel better. I have to go now, but good luck to you; I hope you find what you're looking for. Oh, by the way, make sure you put the garbage back in the right bags when you're done. I want to make it as easy as possible on the garbage men. And whatever you do, don't leave a mess. I don't want to have to come home from work and pick up garbage in the street." Then he shook his head in disbelief.

"Don't worry," said Cane, "you'll find everything just as it was before." Brian, not being rattled by the incident, got in his car and drove off, apparently to work.

Cane mulled it over. *Man, I can't stand that guy. Nothing seems to bother him. He's just too confident; it's funny how nonchalant he is about everything. My garbage trick always works. I've got to keep an eye on him just in case it was he who made the attempt on Rachelle's life.*

Checking in at his office, Cane found a letter on his desk; it was from the president of the company. Philadelphia Mutual was small enough that in a major case like this one, it wouldn't be uncommon for him to deal directly with the man at the top. He sighed and read the note:

Wendell:

As soon as you get in, come to my office and give me the preliminary report on the Rankin case. I need to be up to speed on this one at all times. I need something in writing by the end of the day.

Chad Livingston

Cane sighed again. *I really have no major leads except that credit card bill. I know Livingston is going to want specific details. I know he won't accept the fact that we just might have to pay this one out. If I go tell him that, he'll be furious. I'll just sandbag a little longer and hope for the best. It's better to put off telling him that this one might be a loser.*

Before he could reach the door to go face Livingston, his cell phone rang. He looked at the number and realized it was the call he had been waiting for. He took a deep breath and answered: "Hello? Yes, this is Wendell Cane; yes, I can take the information right now." He ran to his desk, grabbed a piece of paper and began writing energetically as the other person talked. Finally he said, "Are you sure this is accurate? Well, thank you very much. You've been more than helpful. Goodbye, and thanks again."

He hung up the phone and yelled, "Yes! I finally got the break I needed! I knew it." He went to his computer, deleted the preliminary report he had been preparing, and started another one. After a half-hour of heavy typing, he was ready to print, and he felt pleased as he took the hard copy up to Livingston's office.

Livingston's secretary was away from her desk, apparently at lunch. With great news in hand, Cane decided to just knock on Livingston's door unannounced. The door was cracked just a bit, and as he was about to knock, he heard voices on the other side.

Always the nosy investigator, Cane decided to listen. The first thing he heard was Livingston saying, "So what do you think, Bentley?" Cane knew Michael Bentley from meetings; he was one of the vice-presidents under Livingston and apparently a good friend of his.

Bentley said, "I don't know. Are you sure these cuts have to be made?"

"Absolutely," Livingston said. "We have to cut costs to improve the bottom line. You know we have to bring the price of the stock up. I'm retiring in four months; I want to turn my one million in stock options into two million if I can. I get another seven hundred and fifty thousand in a guaranteed cash severance package. When I leave, I want to get everything I can."

He went on, "I'm going to sell my stock and end up with at least three and a half million when it's all said and done. Not only that, but Philadelphia Mutual is going to pay me a guaranteed eighty thousand a year pension as long as I live. And I plan on living a long time. After I'm gone, I don't care what happens to the company. I'll have everything I need."

Bentley said, "I hear you. I'm not retiring that far behind you and my package will be sweet, too. By the way, who are you going to let go?"

"Well, one woman in Accounts Payable, you know, what's her name?"

"Oh. You mean Lindsey Washington."

"Yeah, her. She can get unemployment. She'll find another job anyway. She's still young."

"Who else has to go?" Bentley asked.

"Definitely Cane. He's a great investigator but I'm not letting Kenny go. You and I know he isn't as good as Cane, but I have no choice; he's my son-in-law and I'd never hear the end of it. He's a screw-up, but oh well. After I retire, the last thing I want to hear is my daughter whining to me that her husband doesn't have a job and asking me for money."

"Does it have to be Cane?" Bentley asked.

"Yes, it has to be Cane, and that's final. Do you expect me to cut my own throat before I retire? It's not going to happen. Besides, Cane will manage. He'll get by. He's weird anyway. It's been tough working with him all these years. You know, I hear he has pet rats and kisses them every day. That's just too weird for me. Cane has to go, and my son-in-law stays. There are others who have to go as well, but I haven't finished the list yet."

"When are you going to break the news to these people?" asked Bentley.

Livingston replied, "I'm going to let Miss Washington go really soon, but not Cane until after this case is over. I need him at least until then. Hopefully he's found out something by now. I don't want to give that payout until after I'm retired. If we show that five million dollar loss on our balance sheet, my stock option value could go down. I need all the help I can get. In the worst case, we can delay payment until next quarter and then it won't show up until I'm gone.

"I want you to have severance packages drawn up for both Washington and Cane. Not too generous, the smaller the payout the better. Just give him five thousand for every year worked and unemployment compensation. Also, have their 401(k)s transferred out when they leave. That will hold them for a while.

"By the time we're done," concluded Livingston, "Cane will get well over a hundred thousand and so will Washington. That's plenty for them. They don't need that much money anyway because they're used to living modestly."

Cane couldn't believe his ears. He felt faint. He couldn't fathom that his company was going to do this to him after he had given them twenty loyal years of his life and saved Philadelphia Mutual over fourteen million dollars in claims.

Fury gathered in his mind. *Isn't that the way it always works? I get a lousy hundred thousand after I did most of the work and Livingston gets millions. And worst of all, Livingston's son-in-law gets to stay. He's a bumbling fool. Talk about nepotism; this is nepotism at its finest.* Cane was disgusted; he felt sick to his stomach.

Disgruntled and let down, he returned to his office, crumpling up the preliminary report and throwing it in the trash. He felt fed up with his life. He had always prided himself on doing what was right, and this was the thanks he got for being loyal. Cane knew exactly how Jim Rankin must have felt when he blew up at the customer at his job. Cane had hit his breaking point and was determined to do something about it.

After carefully thinking about what to do, he decided he had no choice but to go back to Livingston's office and confront him. He went back up the hall prepared for the worst and ready to give him a piece of his mind. Livingston let Cane right in, having been expecting him.

Livingston told Cane to sit down and said, "You know Michael Bentley," motioning towards Bentley. "He's been sitting in on my affairs lately. He wants to learn as much about the company as he can. What do you have on the Rankin case?"

Cane was just about to tell Livingston to shove it when an idea popped in his head. *Why don't I just play this thing out and see where it leads? After all, I have the upper hand because I know what Livingston's plans are. He needs me right now because I'm on the biggest case we have had in years. They can't let me go now or they'll have to pay out sooner than they want to. Maybe I can squeeze Livingston and buy some time. People like him hate one thing more than anything: losing money. If I wait it out, maybe something will happen in my favor.*

"Cane. Did you hear me? What's going on in the Rankin case? Do you have the preliminary report?"

"I'm sorry, sir. I've been very busy with this case and I'll have it to you first thing in the morning."

Livingston said, "I want that report on my desk no later than ten o'clock tomorrow morning. Got it?"

"You'll have it, sir. You can count on me."

"Do you know why this is such a big deal to us?" Livingston continued. "Earnings season is coming up and we'd hate to report a loss like that. If you can prove fraud in this one, I see potential mobility in your future with this company."

Cane almost told Livingston off, but he held his tongue. *The gall of this man is beyond belief. How can he lie like that and not think twice about it? Cane, be patient; hang in there. His son-in-law isn't half the investigator you are, and eventually the company will suffer.*

How does he look in the mirror every day? I've lost all respect for this man. And that comment about me kissing my mice is completely wrong. I've never kissed my mice. I like my mice and I play with them. He has no clue who I am or how smart I am. I'll get him back if it's the last thing I do.

He recovered, saying, "Oh, thank you sir, for considering me for a promotion. I knew you had noticed all the hard work I've done over the years. You can count on me. I'll have that report on your desk at ten o'clock sharp, sir."

As he headed back to his office, he thought furiously, *How can he tell me I'll move up in the company when he knows he's going to let me go? He's a total idiot. To think I worked for him all these years. I should sign off on the case right now and declare Rachelle the beneficiary. That would get him. But it really wouldn't do anything for me except get me fired sooner.*

I'm going to take a couple of days off. I haven't missed a day in seven years and it's time. How stupid am I to give all my vacation days back to Philadelphia Mutual? It's going to end with them getting rid of me. I should have known better than to be loyal to them. I don't know how I'm going to get Livingston back or even if I will, but I sure want to...

His face curved into a smile. *Man, is he going to hit the roof when I tell him I want a day off right in the middle of the case. What's the difference, though? They don't care about me. Hearing that conversation between Livingston and Bentley changed my life. From this moment on, I'm going to start living my life to the fullest and I'm going to put my job last. I have one more thing to check out, though. Even though I don't care anymore, I have to know about those charges on Jim's card.*

Back in his office, he spent much of the afternoon writing up a new preliminary report, laughing to himself as he finished it. *You want a report? Well, you got one.* Then he puttered about in his office, thinking about what to do next. He went home that evening very distressed about the fact that he was going to be unemployed in a few weeks.

$ $ $

The next morning, he handed in his report to Livingston just on time, and said, "Of course, this is just a preliminary. Give me a little more time and I think I can find a lead."

Livingston frowned. "I hope you can, for your sake and mine. This tells me nothing."

"Just be patient. Don't I always come through for you?"

"Yeah, I guess you have in the past. Keep me posted on what's going on."

"Yes, sir." He paused, then continued, "I'm going to need this coming Friday and Monday off. I have a sick second cousin who might not make it until next week. This might be my last chance to see him."

Livingston was furious. "Are you kidding me? You want to leave right in the middle of the biggest case we've had in years? I don't think so. Besides, I thought you didn't have any relatives."

"Sir, I haven't had a day off in over seven years and besides, my second cousin is dying. I have this case under control and I really have to go."

Livingston, realizing he needed Cane's cooperation, said, "Fine. You can go, but I want you back here first thing Tuesday morning. This is a big one and I want to postpone payment as long as we can. You know the routine."

"Yes, sir. I'll be back Tuesday morning bright and early, working diligently."

Back in his office, Cane felt rejuvenated. His life had meaning and purpose; he was pleased that for the first time in a long time he had put himself before his job. After that, Cane figured he would make sure his vacation was going to be a special one so he picked up the phone and booked a flight out of town.

After he was done he had a sudden inspiration. *I'm going to round up all my minor claims and push them through. It's the least I can do for our customers; Lord knows I've held back claim money from a lot of people until the last possible moment. My company doesn't care about me, so why should I care about my company? Besides, if they can pay Livingston all that money they must have plenty to go around.*

That afternoon, Cane went up to Livingston's office in hopes of catching him before he left. He knew that Tuesday and Thursday were Livingston's golf days and he always left early. He hoped to get Livingston to sign off on the minor claims before his vacation.

He found Livingston with golf club in hand, just about to putt across the plush carpet into an overturned cup on the other side of the room. Cane said, "Sir, I need to see you a moment."

Livingston snapped, "Can't you see I'm ready to putt? You should know better than to disturb someone getting ready to putt. Just wait a moment."

As he waited, Cane surveyed Livingston's extravagantly outfitted office: the finest leather furniture money could buy; an intercom and expensive stereo system; and a mahogany bar with wine and liquor imported from all over the world. There were large plate glass windows on two sides, offering magnificent views of the city.

Suddenly he was filled with disgust and disdain for Livingston. *This guy does nothing and lives a life of luxury, and he wants to get rid of me to get more money for his retirement. That's ludicrous! I can't wait for him to get what's coming to him.*

Livingston putted and watched eagerly as the ball rolled across the carpet. When it missed the cup, he clenched his teeth, swung the putter wildly and hit the floor with great force. "See? That's why I don't like to be disturbed when I'm practicing. I tee off in less than an hour and I have to get my game together."

Well, maybe if you relaxed and stopped trying to cheat people your game would get better, Cane thought. Aloud he said only, "I'm sorry sir, but I had to see you."

"Well, what do you want?"

"I need you to sign these claims before I go."

"You know I'm in a hurry; can't they wait? Oh, give them to me."

As Livingston was signing the files, Cane said, "I'll see you in a few days."

Livingston looked confused. "Oh, yeah, you're going to see your sick cousin. I want you back on that case first thing Tuesday morning."

"You can count on me, sir. I'm a real company man."

Once outside Livingston's office, Cane grinned as he walked down the hall. *He didn't even look at what he was signing. All he cares about is his golf game. He's definitely in retirement mode.* Satisfaction drifted over him; he wasn't sure if it was because he was taking vacation days or because at last he was truly seeing how Livingston and his company operated.

He hurried to Accounts Payable to finalize the payments. He greeted the processor with a big smile as he always did. This was Lindsey Washington, the other person Livingston meant to eliminate. Lindsey was his own age, forty-one, divorced for ten years with no children. She was short and a little chunky, with dyed blonde hair. Cane had always found her pretty but had never tried to start anything. He opened today with, "So, how's the job going?"

Lindsey said, "It's all right, but sometimes it stinks just like any other job."

Cane moved a little closer and said, "Can you keep a secret?"

"Better than anyone you know."

Cane whispered, "I heard from a very reliable source that the company is going to be cutting back soon. I know there are some layoffs coming."

"It's probably me," said Lindsey. "I'm sure I'd be first on the list. They work me like a dog around here. Sometimes I get three people's work to do. Most days I have to work twelve hours to get everything done and of course they only pay me for eight. I'm sick of it. They always let the good people go and keep the slackers."

Yeah, tell me about it, Cane thought. *Just look at Livingston's son-in-law.* It occurred to him that Lindsey had reached her own breaking point and it was probably good that she was going to be let go. He remembered what had happened to Jim Rankin, and how he himself had felt when he overheard Livingston and Bentley talking about cutbacks.

He said, "I need you to promise that you will not repeat what I'm going to tell you."

"I promise, I won't say a word."

"I overheard Livingston talking and both you and I are going to be let go."

"Oh no. I knew it. What am I going to do?"

"I don't know what either of us is going to do. I was so frustrated at first, but now I'm actually glad. You see, since I realized how this company really is, I feel so much better because I'm living for me now instead of Philadelphia Mutual. It's as if I have a new life."

"But I need this job," said Lindsey.

"They don't care about little people like us, so don't you care about them. Besides, you're going to get severance. Hey listen, do you want to go out and get dinner tonight? I'm going out of town tomorrow and I could really use a friend to talk to. I told you I'm a different person now, so I am not afraid to ask a beautiful woman like you to go to dinner as friends."

Lindsey sat blankly and said hesitantly, "'I don't know. I'm really upset right now about being let go." After a moment's silence she asked, "You want to go to dinner with me, though?"

"Absolutely."

"Okay, I'd love to go. What time do you want to meet?"

"Write down your address and I'll pick you up at six."

"That will be perfect," said Lindsey. "I'm going to leave early anyway. I'm going to let the work back up for once."

"I have one little favor to ask."

"Anything. What is it?"

"Will you see to it that these claims go through for disbursement by tomorrow? It's my one last effort to get these people paid and to get Livingston back."

"No problem," said Lindsey. "I'll see you at six."

When Cane got back to his office, he punched his fist in the air. "Yes! I can't believe I'm really going out on a date. I haven't asked anyone out in twenty years. I'm going to make this night special, one to remember." He got on the phone to some of the finest restaurants in town, and was happy to get a table at a popular, upscale place called The Ready Pheasant.

He spent the rest of the afternoon in a cheerful mood, but when 5:30 finally came, he was nervous. He arrived at Lindsey's at 5:45 and waited outside her apartment. He had always been a little compulsive, and even though he counted himself a changed person, old habits compelled him to be there exactly at 6:00 and not a minute earlier or later.

On the stroke of 6:00, he approached Lindsey's door. He rang the buzzer and heard Lindsey's voice over the intercom. "I'll be right down." After a minute, Lindsey came down, wearing a beautiful dress.

"You . . . you look incredible," said Cane.

Lindsey smiled warmly. "Thank you, Mr. Cane."

"We're going to The Ready Pheasant. Our reservation is for 6:30."

"The Ready Pheasant! Wow, are you sure?"

"Absolutely. I'm going to start living life to the fullest." He walked Lindsey to his car and opened and closed the door for her. As they drove to the restaurant Cane struggled to find words. He was a bit nervous being out with a woman for the first time in what seemed like an eternity. And when they finally got to The Ready Pheasant Cane was glad. The Madre Dee seated the two and Cane pulled the chair out for Lindsey just like a gentleman would.

Cane started by ordering wine. When the waiter brought them each a glass, Cane said, "You know what? Bring us both another glass each. It's a special night. I'm celebrating the new person I've become and the fact that I realize so much of life is ahead of me. Miss Washington is a very special person and she deserves the best."

"Right away, sir."

Lindsey was glowing as she asked, "Did you really mean that?"

"Of course. I wouldn't have said it if I didn't mean it."

"Well, thank you. It's just, well, it's just, you never showed an interest in me before."

Cane looked down and then back to Lindsey, smiling. "I would have, if I hadn't been married to Philadelphia

Mutual. I spent twenty years giving everything I had to that company, and for what? Now I'm middle-aged and I've missed out on so much. If I could do it over, I would. I would've asked you out to dinner years ago." He downed the rest of his glass of wine.

Lindsey said, "Wow, I never knew you were so outgoing and forward."

"I'm not. I've just changed my ways. I mean, look at me. I haven't had a drink in years and here I'm going to be on my second one as soon as the waiter gets here."

"I wondered about that. You don't seem like the drinking type."

"I'm not, but this is a special occasion," Cane said.

"I wish I could be as carefree as you, but I'm worried about getting another job."

"Oh, please," said Cane. "With your work ethic, you'll have another job in no time. Don't worry so much. Let's have a great time tonight and we can deal with our problems tomorrow."

"You know what? You're right." She raised her glass of wine and drained it.

The rest of the evening fell into place; they spent the entire evening laughing and joking. They were two lost souls who had finally met, social outcasts who had never learned what life was about. Now they were finding that so much of life lay ahead for them if they would just give up their unconfident ways.

The evening was so magical that Cane didn't want it to end, but he had a plane to catch in the morning, so he told Lindsey he had to go. When he walked Lindsey up to her apartment, he said, "Thank you for one of the greatest evenings of my life."

Lindsey said, "Hopefully there will be many more," and kissed him on the cheek. "Good night, Wendell, and have a safe trip." And she went inside.

As he left, Cane was on top of the world. He had never been in a real relationship, and that was the first time a woman had kissed him. That night he went to bed feeling high-spirited from the wonderful evening, and he didn't even think about the Rankin case.

CHAPTER 9

ane got up early the next morning and rushed to get to the airport. On the way, thoughts of the tremendous night before echoed in his mind. In the airport parking lot, he mused, *All these years I've been slaving away, and for what? I've missed out on the best years of my life. I like Lindsey, and when I get back I'm going to ask her out again. I'm not a very good-looking guy, but maybe she can see past that. I can't wait to see her again.*

He went into the airport, passed through security, and eventually boarded his plane. When he arrived at his seat, there was a very heavy man sitting in it. Cane said, "Excuse me, sir. You're in my seat."

The man said, "Is it all right if we trade seats? Mine is the window seat, and I like to be in the aisle."

"Well, that isn't happening. I have the aisle seat, so please move."

"Come on, simpleton," the man said. "A little guy like you will fit OK in the window seat. Just sit down."

Cane had been an aggravator for most of his adult life. He knew exactly how to get under someone's skin without going too far. He said, "For the last time, please get out of my seat or I'll be forced to get the flight attendant and have you moved. I'm sure if the entire staff on the plane worked together they could probably help you up."

The heavy man stood up cumbersomely and said, "I should—"

Cane interrupted loudly, "You should what?"

The man saw that the flight attendant was coming to see what the disturbance was about, and said, "I should take my seat." He squeezed into the window seat looking very uncomfortable.

The flight attendant walked up and said, "Is there a problem here?"

Cane said, "Oh no, there's no problem. I was just helping this man find his seat."

"Oh, how nice of you. If all our passengers were as helpful as you, all our flights would be great."

"Thanks for the compliment." He glanced at the heavy man, who looked angry.

Suddenly Cane felt great. He had always done what was to his benefit while outsmarting the other person. It was a novel insight: *I know that's the way it works. You just stand up for yourself and then you get acclaim from the people in charge. I always knew that the person that backs down always gets burned.* He settled in comfortably, thinking, *This is going to be a great trip. I can't wait to forget about Philadelphia Mutual for a few days. I'm going to spend a few hours working on that new lead as soon as I get off the plane, and then it's all rest and relaxation.*

After he finished a few hours of investigating, he spent the rest of the next three days all by himself. He forgot all about his problems and didn't even turn on his cell phone. It was a great time and a great relief to just kick back and relax. He took an overnight flight home on Sunday and arrived mid-day Monday.

$$\$ \ \$ \ \$$$

While Cane was on his way home from the airport, Rachelle was preparing to go to the grocery store with Curt. As they walked towards Curt's car, a white van with tinted windows sped up towards them; the passenger side window of the van suddenly rolled down and a man pointed a gun out of it. Rachelle screamed, "Get down!"

They dove for cover behind a car just as gunfire rang out, but Rachelle fell to the ground with a bullet in her shoulder. She groaned in pain as several other shots went wildly by them.

Curt pulled out his handgun as the van stopped in front of their car. He yelled to Rachelle, "Stay down!" He fired two shots into the air, avoiding the van.

Someone in the van yelled, "They got a gun! Let's get out of here." The van raced away with its tires squealing. As it sped away, it ran a red light at the first intersection. An oncoming car clipped the van's rear passenger side. The van fishtailed, spun wildly for a moment, hit a parked car just past the light, slid down the street and finally slammed into another parked car. The front end was completely flattened, the van was in ruins.

A passerby ran up and shouted, "Are you two all right?" While he was trying to open the driver's side door, the van's occupants leaped out of the passenger side door. The shooter yelled to the driver, "Let's get out of here," and they took off on foot.

Another man ran up and asked, "Is everyone all right?"

The shooter shouted, "Don't follow us or I'll put a bullet in your head." The driver, who was trying to keep up with the shooter, was limping noticeably and bleeding from a gash on his face. A crowd quickly gathered, the assailants escaping on foot as they watched.

Curt stood over Rachelle yelling, "Someone help, please someone help! Someone call an ambulance." He was beginning to tremble.

A bystander ran up and said, "I'll call for an ambulance. You stay with her."

Curt knelt next to Rachelle and tried to attend to her. She was bleeding fairly heavily, the blood forming a puddle on the concrete. He stripped off his shirt and applied pressure to the wound, saying, "You'd better not die on me. You'd better not die on me."

"Everything seems so cold," murmured Rachelle.

The bystanders did all they could to help; one gave up his coat while another brought a blanket from inside. Curt carefully covered Rachelle to keep her warm and to prevent her from going into shock. When she tried to talk, Curt cut her off, saying shakily, "Don't try to talk. Save your strength. An ambulance is on the way. Stay with me, babe! Please stay with me!"

A few minutes later the police and an ambulance arrived; two paramedics rushed to Rachelle's side. After stabilizing the bleeding, they loaded her in the ambulance. Curt demanded and was allowed to ride to the hospital with Rachelle, while the police questioned the eyewitnesses.

In the ambulance, Curt kept talking to Rachelle to keep her spirits up: "Come on Rachelle, stay with me. You're a fighter, just like me. Don't give up."

Seven minutes later at County Hospital, Rachelle was rushed into the operating room where doctors worked feverishly to prevent her from losing any more blood.

Munson was notified about the incident and rushed to the hospital to question Curt. He phoned Cane, who had just arrived home and was unpacking his things. "Cane. It's Munson. Rachelle Johnson was just shot and was taken to the hospital. I don't have any details on how severe it is yet. She's in the operating room now. I assume it was another attempted hit. I'm on my way right now; how long before you can get over to County?"

"I'm leaving now," said Cane. He hung up, went out to his car and headed for the hospital.

When Cane arrived, Munson was already questioning Curt; he stepped out briefly to fill Cane in on what had happened. He noted, "I've been questioning Curt for about ten minutes now, and the entire time, he's been pacing back and forth."

"Yeah," said Cane, "I wonder if he really is concerned for her health, or if all he cares about is the money?"

"I don't know about that. He does seem to care about her. Let's go ask him a few more questions."

They went back in to see Curt. Munson said, "I know I already asked you this, but are you sure you didn't get a good look at the shooter?"

Curt said snidely, "No, I didn't get a good look at the shooter. But I'm telling you, if anything happens to Rachelle I'm going to take care of those guys who did this to her."

"I know you're upset," said Munson, "but if you know what's good for you, you'll let us do our job and handle this. If you retaliate, you'll end up in jail and you'll be no better than the people that did this. Trust me, it's not worth it. Besides, you're in enough trouble as it is."

"Why would I be in trouble?"

"Well, I'll let you know if we're going to be filing charges against you."

"You want to file charges against *me*? That's crazy! I was the one who was almost killed because you refused to provide us with police protection, remember? Well, it almost cost both Rachelle and me our lives. I had to defend myself because you wouldn't help."

"You were carrying an illegal handgun and, whether you were fired upon or not, it's still illegal. And since you fired it in public, you could be charged with a serious crime."

"Wait a minute," said Curt. "Shouldn't you be out finding the people who did this? You're treating me like a criminal when I'm the victim."

"You don't get it, do you?" Munson asked. "If you had accidentally shot and killed an innocent bystander, you could go to jail for manslaughter even if you were trying to defend yourself. Think about it. I'll talk to the city attorney's office and see what we can do about letting you slide on the weapons charge, but I don't know."

"You do that," said Curt. "Because I'll beat that charge for sure. Plus, I don't know if you want it in the newspapers that we begged for protection and you refused to give it to us. I don't think you want the public to know that the police aren't willing to protect them."

Munson frowned. "There's no need to get nasty. I'll do what I can. In the meantime, I'll make a phone call and see about getting twenty-four hour protection to watch over Ms. Johnson, just to be certain there isn't another attempt on her life. Right now, just try to relax. I'm sure that she'll be fine."

"She'd better be."

"I guess that's everything here," Munson concluded. "You'll have to come down to the station and sign your formal statement. I want to let you know that I'll do everything in my power to bring the people who did this to justice. Let me know the minute you know anything. I have to go now, so take care."

Curt was surprised that Munson seemed genuinely concerned. Just then the surgeon came into the waiting room. Munson said, "Oh no. I hope it isn't bad news."

The doctor walked up to Curt and said, "Mr. Clark, I'm Dr. Kenzie. I operated on Miss Johnson." He glanced at Munson and Cane, and Curt nodded to give the doctor approval to speak in front of the two investigators.

Dr. Kenzie said, "I have good news for you. Miss Johnson is going to be just fine. The bullet struck her in the shoulder just to the left of an artery. We had to repair the triceps muscle. It really isn't that serious; the reason it looked so bad when it happened was that she did lose a lot of blood on that sidewalk, and also, she was in shock.

"In fact, the bullet struck one of the least dangerous places it could have. A little further right, and it might have struck an artery and she could have bled to death. Consider her to be one lucky individual. She should be able to go home in a couple of days and make a full recovery. Before long, she'll just have a scar and a bad memory to remind her of this whole ordeal. You probably can see her in a few hours. She'll be a little groggy at first, but that will pass."

"Can I see her now, Dr. Kenzie?"

"I guess you could for a minute, but only a minute; she needs to rest."

The doctor summoned a nurse who escorted Curt into the recovery room. There Rachelle lay unconscious, with an IV in her arm and a heart monitor hooked up. When Curt saw her lying there helplessly, a lump rose in his throat. He felt sorry for her and blamed himself for not protecting her. He also felt guilty for leading her on and having another woman on the side. Curt's feelings for Angel were not as strong as they once were and he found himself wondering if he was actually falling for Rachelle. They had had a couple of years of nothing more than a friendship and a physical relationship to satisfy each other's needs.

Curt said quietly, "Rachelle? Can you hear me?"

Rachelle didn't respond and lay there listlessly from the anesthetic.

"You have to go now," the nurse said. "Just let her rest and we'll let you know the moment she wakes up. She should be fine in a few hours. You're welcome to sit in the waiting room if you like. I can guarantee you won't get to see her for at least four hours, though. I suggest you go home and get some rest. I know it's been a very traumatic situation for you. You might be better off coming back later instead of punishing yourself by waiting."

An armed police officer pulled a chair up just outside the recovery room and sat down. The nurse continued, "I'll tell you what. You go home and get some rest and come back at six o'clock and I'll personally get you in to see her."

"Maybe you're right," said Curt. "It won't do any good for me to stay here. I have something I have to do that can't wait, anyway."

The nurse said, "Now you're thinking straight. I'll see you at six."

On leaving the hospital, Curt drove straight to Angel's house. He hadn't seen her much since the first attempt on Rachelle's life, having spent most of his time trying to keep Rachelle safe.

When Angel opened the door, she went to kiss Curt, but he pulled away.

"What's wrong?" she asked. "Are you trying to break up with me?"

"No, I'm not breaking up with you. It's just that I was almost killed and I'm all shaken up."

"What happened?" Angel cried, misty-eyed.

Curt explained the entire incident and told her that the police would be watching him very closely now. He sighed because he knew what he was going to do next wouldn't go over well; Angel was young and sensitive. He began, "I'm lucky to be alive, so I need you to be strong and not cry. You have to trust me when I say that I can't see you for a while. If I'm seen with you, it could mess everything up. There could be no five million dollars, no record deal and no future for us. I can't see you until further notice."

Angel began to cry. "But I love you."

"I know you do, baby, but I'm confused right now. It's going to be just as hard for me as it is for you, but I can't take the chance." He pushed her into the apartment, shut the door and began kissing her passionately.

"I trust you," said Angel.

They kissed passionately again, but Curt pulled away. "I can't do this. I have to go now. I'll be in touch; try not to contact me in the next few days unless it's an emergency." And he walked out the door, leaving Angel upset, and headed back to the hospital to wait to see Rachelle.

Meanwhile, Cane and Munson headed back to the police station where all the witnesses had already given their statements. Two witnesses had gotten a good look at the suspects and were busy looking at mug shots, trying to come up with a positive identification of the assailants.

The police artist came in to see Munson and said, "Check this out. The pictures from each witness look almost identical. Usually people have different perspectives and see the perpetrator differently. This time we drew them real close."

Munson surveyed the sketches. "Get copies of these out right away to the entire force; we'll need an all points bulletin. The sooner we bring these guys in, the better. Go on, make it snappy."

At the end of the long day, Munson was displeased that neither witness had had any luck positively identifying the suspects. He released the witnesses and asked them to pick up where they left off on the mug books the following day.

It was now evening, and Curt was finally going to get a chance to see Rachelle. Shortly after six, the nurse took him to Rachelle's room. Rachelle was awake and lying on her back.

Curt said, "Hi, babe. How are you?"

"Wow, this pain medication is good stuff," Rachelle said, "but I can still feel the incision a little."

"I'm so sorry, Rachelle, that I didn't see it coming. I should've been more observant, especially after the first attempt. If anything happened to you, I just don't know what I'd do. I promise I'll make them pay for what they did to you."

Rachelle said weakly, "No. Don't do anything stupid. The policeman outside the door told me they have two reliable witnesses who'll be able to identify the men who did this. They're going to catch these guys and once they link them to that devil woman Godzilla, she'll be toast. She'll be out of our hair for good. Besides, don't forget about the five million. Promise me, for the first time in your life you won't do anything stupid. Please let the police handle it."

Curt shook his head in discontent. "Well, they'd better catch them soon because I can't stand to see you lying here like this. If the police don't catch them right away, I'll find out who they are and go after them myself."

"Curt, I know how your temper is, so I want you to promise me you won't do anything, no matter what. Now promise."

"All right, I promise, but they'd better find them soon. I don't trust that idiot detective they have on this case. I don't know how that guy ever graduated from the police academy."

The nurse came in and said to Rachelle, "How are you doing?"

"It hurts a little, but mostly I just want to sleep," Rachelle said.

"The wound wasn't that severe, but you never can be sure," the nurse said. "I'll tell you what. Why don't you go home and let her get some sleep? It's the best thing for her right now. You can come back tomorrow and I'm sure you'll see a great improvement after the medication wears off." Her expression said that he had no choice but to leave, because she wasn't going to let him stay.

Curt said, "All right. I'll be back tomorrow morning." He leaned over the bed, kissed her forehead and hugged her gently, adding for the first time, "I love you." Rachelle, caught off guard, didn't respond. He left the room without saying another word.

Curt now realized he was in a heap of trouble; he had told two women that he loved them. He loved Angel, but now he was falling for Rachelle as well, and was faced with the wrath of one woman if he stayed with the other. This predicament would surely end in disaster. *I don't know what I'm going to do. I think I love Rachelle more than Angel. I'm going to have to make a decision soon, and no matter what, I'm going to lose.*

His mind raced as it had all day long. He went home exhausted and lay down to sleep, but even as he dozed off, the thoughts kept coming. *I don't know what to do. I guess I'll just have to string them both along until something gives. I can't leave Rachelle after we get the money. We almost lost our lives today and I think I love her.*

He fell asleep with one last thought in his head: *I can't leave Rachelle now. I just can't.*

CHAPTER 10

The next morning, both witnesses returned to the police station to continue going through the mug books. After two hours of looking, one of the witnesses asked to see Detective Munson. The witness pointed to one of the pictures, saying, "This was the driver of the vehicle."

"Are you absolutely sure he was the driver?"

"I have no doubt. I'm one hundred percent sure."

"Bring the other witness in to confirm this," Munson said to Detective Ramsey.

When the other witness was brought in, Munson said, "There are thirty-two photos on the page I'm about to show you. I want you to tell me if any of them look like either of the people in the van you saw the other day."

The other witness looked at the page carefully and said, "That's the man right there. That's the guy who jumped out and ran away with a limp. I'm absolutely sure of it."

Munson grabbed the book, turned to Ramsey, and said, "Put out an all points bulletin on Bruno Slaggert. Check for last known addresses. If you find him, get a couple of the guys to go with you and pick him up for questioning. I think Mr. Slaggert just might be the break I've been looking for. And get me his rap sheet. I want it on my desk in ten minutes!" Detective Ramsey nodded and immediately left the room.

Minutes later, Ramsey came back with a folder and said, "Here's Slaggert's rap sheet. He's quite a guy. I'm surprised he's still on the street. I have two cars ready to go over to his last known address right now. I've got a couple extra guys because he could be dangerous."

Munson nodded in approval. "Good work, Ramsey."

After Ramsey left, Munson grabbed the file on Slaggert and sat down. *Let's see*, Munson thought. *Pick-pocketing when he was sixteen years old, got a slap on the wrist; shoplifting six months later, probation; drug possession at seventeen, thirty days at the youth home; breaking and entering at nineteen. That was his first adult offense so he got probation, then another breaking and entering at twenty-one, a year in upstate prison; minor in possession at twenty-two, another year at upstate; receiving stolen goods at twenty-five, charges dropped. A career criminal. If I can get this guy to turn in his friend, I'll have a solid attempted murder charge. I'll get him if it's the last thing I do.*

A little while later, Detective Ramsey and four uniformed officers arrived at Slaggert's dilapidated house, which was in one of the most crime-ridden areas in the city. When Ramsey knocked on the door, Slaggert opened it a crack. Ramsey said, "Are you Bruno Slaggert? Come on out; we have some questions we want to ask you."

Slaggert had the door chain-locked and tried to slam it shut; one of the officers jammed it with his foot. Slaggert galloped through his house and bolted out the back door. The police officers kicked the door in; two of the officers ran through Slaggert's house chasing after him, while the other two and Ramsey jumped into separate cars to pull around the block just behind Slaggert's house. Slaggert had a head start and was able to jump the fence into the neighbor's yard behind his house. He crossed the street, hopped another fence and came out two blocks away from his own house.

The two officers chasing him on foot were in hot pursuit and gaining ground. Meanwhile, the two police cars pulled down the adjoining streets, hoping to spot him. Ramsey picked up his two-way radio and said, "This is Detective Ramsey. I need at least two more cars in the area of Madison and Vine. In pursuit of suspect Bruno Slaggert, five feet ten inches tall, brown hair, was last seen wearing blue jeans and a brown shirt. Suspect last seen on Harrison Street on foot, I repeat headed towards Madison and Vine with two uniformed officers in pursuit."

The dispatcher responded with, "Copy. Help is on the way."

Two streets over, Ramsey spotted Slaggert running into another yard, limping slightly but moving fast. He called over the radio, "Suspect headed south towards Beech Street cutting through yards. I'll go four streets over. Phillips and Callaway, you go three streets over and try and intercept him on Russet."

Phillips responded, "Yes, sir." His car pulled up on Russet and Callaway jumped out, telling his partner Phillips, "Circle the block and if you don't see him, come back. I'm going to hide over there by that driveway. Go!"

Callaway positioned himself out of sight, and soon heard Slaggert running in his direction and panting hard. He peered around the corner to verify that it was Slaggert, pulled out his billy club and waited. As Slaggert ran by, Callaway swung his club low, catching Slaggert in the shins. Slaggert yelled in pain, tumbled over and slid a few feet on the cement.

Callaway pounced on him and held him down, yelling, "Don't move." Slaggert, dazed and hurting, merely moaned. The other two officers Cranston and Wilson ran up on foot, out of breath, and helped hold Slaggert down as Callaway handcuffed him. A second later Phillips' and Ramsey's police cars raced up and screeched to a stop. Ramsey got out of the car and came up and said, "Good work, men. Put him in the back of my car. Callaway, you ride with me down to the station. Munson is going to have a field day with this guy."

Slaggert whined, "You hurt my sore leg. That's police brutality."

"Your leg couldn't have been that sore the way you hopped those fences. It's surprising what people can do when they're being chased."

Right when Ramsey got in the car, he radioed his dispatcher to tell Munson that they had the suspect in custody. When Munson heard this he dialed Cane's number. "Cane, you'd better get down here right away. I think we have the driver. All right, I'll see you when you get here."

Cane arrived at the station shortly after that and went up to Crosby and said, "Is Munson in?"

"Hey, Cane, you greasy slug. When I first saw you, I thought you were a criminal being brought in for questioning. It's hard to tell the difference between you and a common thief."

"Yeah, when I walked in and saw you, I thought I walked into a jail cell by mistake. Oh and by the way, I see you put on more weight. You're almost up to your goal of size fifty-two pants. They both laughed, and then Cane said, "Hey, is Munson here?"

"Yeah, he's back there somewhere. He hasn't been in a good mood lately so don't get on his nerves. Man, that man is a workaholic. Go on back."

Slaggert was brought in as Munson was briefing Cane. The two followed Ramsey into the interrogation room and Ramsey got right to the point. "All right, Slaggert. This is the deal. We have two witnesses who will positively identify you as the driver of a white van where a shooter almost killed a woman. They even described your head injury from the crash. This is going to be an open and shut case.

"We have you on accessory to attempted murder, resisting arrest, fleeing the scene of an accident, grand theft auto and probably conspiracy to commit murder. With your record, you're looking at ten to twenty years. And you don't look like the type who would fare well in prison with all those hardened criminals. With what we have on you, you won't be going to any upstate prison like you did before. You'll probably be doing time in Albertson and, let me tell you, those guys up there like young guys like you."

"Yeah, we'll see," said Slaggert. "This is America and I'm innocent until proven guilty. I'm not answering any questions until I speak to a lawyer."

"Yeah, yeah," said Munson, "you can have your phone call right after we do the lineup. When we knew you were going to be picked up, we arranged for the witnesses to be ready to go when you got here. The doctor'll get you cleaned up and then off you go."

When the doctor was finished with Slaggert, Munson led the suspect to a small room with a one-way mirror. Five other men were already waiting there. Munson announced over the intercom, "I want you to all line up under a number from one to six." All the suspects took their places under a number. Munson had them face the mirror, face left and face right and finally announced, "All right, everyone exit except Slaggert."

He put Slaggert back in the interrogation room, leaving him to sit alone and grow nervous. Ramsey came up and said, "We have a positive ID from both of them. We got him."

"Excellent. I'm going to squeeze this guy like an orange at a juice factory. By the end of the day, he'll wish he was never born."

He went with Cane and Ramsey into the interrogation room. Slaggert immediately clamored, "I know my rights. I want to see my lawyer. You can't question me until I see my lawyer."

"You know," replied Munson, "all you did was drive. You're willing to go to jail for at least ten years just because you drove a van? You didn't do the shooting, but fine. You want your lawyer, you got him. Trust me, you're going to need him." He unlocked a drawer, pulled out a telephone and plugged it in, and said, "Make your call. We'll be right outside."

After Slaggert's brief phone call, the investigators returned and Munson began with, "All right. When will your lawyer be here?"

"I can't afford an attorney. I need a court appointed one."

Munson smiled, knowing that Slaggert's chances of beating the rap had just severely declined. He turned to Ramsey and said, "Call over to the public defender's office and see if you can get someone down here. The longer I wait, the less I'm willing to do for him. Get him his lawyer. Oh and call the D.A.'s office, too. "

While Ramsey made his calls, Munson sat thinking about the case. *This guy doesn't know what he's in for. All those lawyers down at the public defender's office are extremely over-burdened and grossly underpaid. He'll be lucky if they talk to him for more than ten minutes. They'll probably raise the white flag and tell him to plea bargain when they find out what we have on him. This guy will have to turn state's evidence.*

After an hour's wait, the public defender appeared and Munson said, "Are you kidding me? I can't believe they sent you over, Crungent."

The attorney said to Cane, "I don't believe we've met."

"My name is Wendell Cane. I'm an insurance investigator looking into a payout on the woman who was almost killed."

"I'm Kenneth Crungent with the public defender's office. I see you know Munson."

"Yeah, for many years now."

Crungent said, "I'm sorry to hear that. If you investigate the way Munson does, you probably don't care about people's rights." Cane didn't reply and Crungent continued, "I see Munson has been questioning my client. I'm sure he's already violated at least two or three of his civil rights by now."

Munson said, "You're right, Crungent. Aren't you always right?" At Crungent's dirty look, he added, "I do everything by the book."

"Yeah, your own book. You seem to forget about a little document called the Constitution. That's okay, though, because when you do forget, it makes my job easier. If I find out you violated his rights, I'll have the charges dropped. We've been over this before."

"You guys are all alike," Munson said. "All you want is to put criminals back on the street. What about the victims? When you guys put all these people who should be locked up back in society, innocent people get hurt. I guess victims don't have rights."

"I care about everyone's rights, whether they've been accused of a crime or not. With you around violating everyone's rights all the time, even criminals are the victims."

"Whatever," said Munson.

Crungent continued, "I care more about people than you do. That's why I do a lot of my work *pro bono*, you know, for free. And that's why I have a job where I work eighty hours a week and never get to see my kids. I do it to help people."

"You think you're the only one who puts in eighty hours in a week?" Munson said. "I haven't seen one of my kid's soccer games all season. The difference is that I do it to keep the streets safe and you do it to put criminals back on the street so they're unsafe. That's the big difference between you and me. I guess I shouldn't complain; we have this guy dead to rights and he isn't getting off. He'll need all the help he can get. We got him good."

"I'll be the judge of that," Crungent said. "What have you got?" After a few moments' of perusing the file Munson handed him, he sighed and asked, "Where's Slaggert? Let me see him."

"Questioning room four. Good luck." Crungent gave Munson a dirty look and went to find his client.

In room four, Crungent said, "I'm Kenneth Crungent from the public defender's office and I'll be your attorney. Well, Mr. Slaggert, one thing you need to know about me is that I tell it like it is and I don't candy-coat anything. You, Mr. Slaggert, are in quite a predicament. What were you thinking? Wait, I don't want to know. They have two eye-witnesses who can put you in that van, and with six prior arrests, it doesn't look good. We can try to go to trial, but that might end up getting you ten to twenty. They're going to charge you with accessory to commit murder, grand theft auto, resisting arrest and fleeing the scene of an accident. I can talk to the district attorney and see what he'll do for us. He might want to work out a deal."

Slaggert said, "Talk to him and see if you can get me off."

"Fine, I'll be right back."

Ten minutes later, Crungent was back. "All right, this is the deal. In my opinion, you're up a creek without a paddle. If you go to trial, the D.A. is going to want the maximum sentence. If you plead guilty to the resisting arrest charge, they're willing to drop the accessory to commit murder charge and all the other ones with an agreement of a minimum of six months jail time. In return, they want you to turn state's evidence on the shooter and the people who hired you. Munson knows you didn't do this on your own. I think you'd be crazy not to take it."

Slaggert said, "I want no jail time at all."

"Listen," argued Crungent, "they have you on a ten-to-twenty-year charge. I tried for no jail time and he wouldn't take it. This is a more than generous offer."

Slaggert thought for a minute and said, "All right. I'll take it. The only thing is that I don't know the names of the people who hired us."

"Don't worry about that. I'll talk to Munson and the D.A."

Crungent left and came back a half-hour later with a set of papers. "Here's the deal, ready to sign. I just want to remind you that once you do, you have to cooperate fully. No turning back."

"Yeah, I know. Where do I sign?"

"Right here," said Crungent. Slaggert signed the papers and Crungent quickly took them away. He returned with Cane and Ramsey and said, "All right. Let's get to work. The first thing we want is the name and the address of the shooter who was in the van with you."

Slaggert hesitated, then said, "The guy who did the shooting was Craig Belson. He lives at 4218 Lexington Drive, apartment number 17. Over in Trenton. He doesn't live in the city."

Munson wrote that down and turned to Ramsey and said, "Send a few men over to pick him up for questioning.

It's still within our jurisdiction." As Ramsey left, he went on, "Now, I know you didn't just decide to get up in the morning and go shoot at some random person, so who hired you?"

"It was a man and a woman who hired us. The man gave us ten thousand up front and said he'd pay another seventy-five thousand when the job was done."

Munson laid out pictures of Seth, Brian and Bridget. "Is the man one of these people, and do you know the woman?"

Slaggert looked at the pictures. "That was the woman who hired us, but neither of those guys was the man."

"Are you sure?"

"Yeah, I'm sure. The guy who hired us was well-dressed and had dark hair. That's definitely her, though. She seemed real cold to me."

"What do you mean by 'cold'?"

"Well, she just seemed like she thought she was better than us. And she didn't like Rachelle Johnson one bit. She said she couldn't wait until it was done."

Munson said again, "You're sure that wasn't the guy she was with?"

"I'm telling you, that wasn't him."

Munson looked at Cane and said, "I thought it would be Seth for sure."

Slaggert elaborated. "This guy was an arrogant sucker about five feet ten inches tall. Well-dressed. He didn't look like much, but he did have that chick wrapped around his finger, though. The way she looked at him and followed his every move, she was whipped."

"I think I know who our man is," said Cane. "When I was surveilling Bridget, she met with a man I didn't recognize. She was all over him as if she were in love, believe it or not. At that point, I figured she was just using Seth. I have the guy's address." He wrote it down and gave it to Munson.

"Good work, Cane," laughed Munson. "Now I remember why I always let you hang around here. I'm going to have Bridget Bartkowski, this guy, Seth Rankin, Brian Williams, and Craig Belson all picked up to sort this out. I see a conspiracy to commit murder charge in Ms. Bartkowski's future."

Later that day, Craig Belson was positively identified in the lineup by the witnesses as the other man in the van. He immediately asked for a lawyer and insisted on his innocence. Munson and the D.A. had no plans to make a deal with Belson; they felt confident that with Slaggert's testimony and the positive IDs, they could put Belson away for at least ten years.

When Belson's attorney told him that Slaggert was going to turn state's evidence, Belson snarled, "I'm going to get Slaggert if it's the last thing I do. I'm going to prove I'm innocent. He's gonna pay for this." He threw his chair against the wall, raging that he was innocent and demanding to go to trial. Belson's attorney gave up and left the room until he calmed down.

Meanwhile, four officers went to Bridget's house and knocked on her door. Opening it, she acted surprised. "Are you here to collect for the Policeman's Ball?"

"No, ma'am. We need you to come down to the station and answer some questions about an attempted murder that happened in the city two days ago."

Bridget became angry and said, "I'll do no such thing. You're not taking me anywhere."

"Ma'am, either you can come with us now or we can come back with a warrant and take you in involuntarily. It's your choice."

"I'll come with you," said Bridget, "but you'll be hearing from my attorney about a lawsuit." She complained all the way down to the station until she was put into the line-up room with four other women. Munson put Slaggert behind the one-way glass this time, hoping he would identify Bridget as one of the people who hired him.

When Munson called out, "Ladies, can you all get in line under a number, please," all four of the women lined up except Bridget, who yelled, "This is ridiculous. I'm not a criminal and I refuse to do this." She shook her fist at the mirror.

Slaggert said, "That's definitely her, the mouthy one. Man, is she a witch. She's the kind of woman who'd make a guy shoot himself if he was married to her. I'll never forget her as long as I live."

Munson said, "Are you sure?"

"Are you kidding me? No one who ever met that lady could ever forget her. Yes, I'm sure."

Detective Munson brought Bridget into an interrogation room with Ramsey and Cane. Bridget demanded, "I want to know what this is all about. You brought me down here and treated me like a common criminal. My lawyer is going to slap you with a harassment suit."

"Funny," said Munson, "that's the fourth time I've heard that today. What's wrong with you people? Do you think I'm scared of idle threats? You're in a lot of trouble,

Ms. Bartkowski. You're going to be charged with conspiracy to commit murder. We have a witness who's going to turn state's evidence against you and your boyfriend. This person says you hired him to kill Rachelle Johnson. Is this true?"

"I'm not saying a word until I talk to my lawyer," Bridget said. "Every time you say something, I'm just going to put up my hand and say talk to the hand."

Munson slammed his fist on the table and said, "I've had twelve-years-olds in here who were more mature than that. You think you're smart, don't you? Well, see this piece of paper? It is a sworn statement incriminating you for conspiracy to commit murder. If you don't cooperate, I'll request that the D.A. goes for the maximum sentence, which is fifteen years."

Bridget said, "Let me get this straight. You're going to convict me with the testimony of a well-known felon, when I'm an upstanding citizen without even a speeding ticket on my record? Good luck with that one. My lawyer will have a field day in court."

"I have plenty of evidence. I have motive, which is five million dollars in insurance money. I even have your boyfriend on his way in right now. What do you think of that?"

"Talk to the hand. I'm not saying a word until I talk to my lawyer. What part of that don't you understand?"

"Fine! Have it your way! When the judge hands you a fifteen-year sentence and you're whining about it. I'm just going to hold my hand up and say, 'Talk to the hand.'" He stalked out and slammed the door behind him.

As Cane and Ramsey went to follow him, Cane turned and said, "You'd better think about cooperating. I don't think you'll do well in prison."

"Get out of here, you weird little twit," said Bridget. "They don't have jack on me."

Out in the hall, Munson said, "Man, Slaggert was right. She is a witch. You say she was married to Jim Rankin for a year? The poor guy. It's amazing he didn't commit suicide. I'm going to punish myself and try one more time with her."

After letting her stew a few moments, Munson went back in and said to Bridget, "Listen. I'm going to give you one more chance to cooperate with us. Where were you last Tuesday at four in the afternoon?"

Bridget said, "I was at the new James Bond movie by myself. I couldn't wait to see it. I have the ticket stub at home that will prove it. The usher will remember me as well because I made a complaint that the kids in front of us, I mean in front of me, were making out. It was distracting so I went and got the usher. One of the kids got in an argument with him and ended up leaving. You can check it out. The theater is over on Drexel Street. I think the usher's name was Charles."

Munson said sarcastically, "You complained about something? I just can't imagine you complaining about anything."

Bridget gave Munson a dirty look. "You know what? Just talk to the hand. I want my lawyer. I have one of the best lawyers in the state."

"You'll get your lawyer, "Munson said. "And I'm going to have your story checked out right now." He picked up the phone and ordered an officer out to the theater. As he hung up, an officer burst in and said, " Sir, Rick Emery is here for questioning. We just brought him in."

Bridget looked amazed. Cane said, "Oh, does it surprise you, Ms. Bartkowski, that we know about Mr. Emery and yourself? I followed you and saw you at the park. I guess you're taking both Rick and Seth for a ride."

"You little weasel!" Bridget said. "Who do think you are, following me? Your name should be Weasel instead of Wendell. Weasel Cane — that sounds much better."

Cane said, "Very funny. Don't worry. We didn't say anything to Seth yet. I'm sure he'll be pleased when he finds out how you used him."

"You can't intimidate me and you certainly can't blackmail me. You'd be wise not to say anything else."

"Why? Are you going to put a hit out on me like you did Rachelle?" Cane said.

"I'm not saying another word until I see my lawyer."

They left her there and went to interrogate Rick Emery, whom Slaggert had just identified as the one who hired him. Munson introduced himself and said, "Mr. Emery, do you know why you're here?"

"No, I don't know," Emery said. "Maybe I forgot to pay a parking ticket ten years ago and you're finally catching up with me."

"Oh, we have another smart-aleck on our hands do we? Well, I'll tell you. You're here because we believe you hired a man named Bruno Slaggert to kill Rachelle Johnson."

"Who? I never heard of her," Emery confidently said. "You've obviously made a huge mistake. It's all right, though. We all make mistakes." Emery stood up and said,

"I'll just be on my way now so you can focus on bringing in the right person."

"Sit down," said Munson, "you aren't going anywhere. You seem pretty confident, but we have a sworn statement from Mr. Slaggert saying that you hired him to kill Miss Johnson. He also positively identified you in the lineup. What do you think of that?"

Emery said, "He must be mistaken. Habitual criminals will say anything to get off from a crime they committed. What did you offer him, immunity? That's why he probably lied. I'm an upstanding citizen and he's a common criminal. Who do you think a jury will believe?"

"I see you think you're smarter than everyone else in the world," Munson said. "Since you're so smart, tell me how ten to twenty years in prison sounds."

"It sounds long. I hope you catch the real criminal. I'm sure when you do, the streets will be a safer place and maybe you'll win an award or something."

"Listen here, you idiot," said Munson angrily. "I've been dealing with people like you my whole life. I'm going to make this charge stick, and when it does I'm going to tell the D.A. that you were uncooperative and recommend he ask for hard time in prison."

"If you think I'm involved with this, then you need to go back to the police academy. You must have been out sick when they were teaching you how to solve crimes."

Munson had reached his breaking point. "You little puke! How dare you talk to me like that? I'm going to teach you a lesson in respect." He stood up and Ramsey jumped up and grabbed his arm, saying, "Control yourself, Dennis. He isn't worth it. We've got him on conspiracy to commit murder. He won't last five minutes in prison. Don't ruin our case."

Munson took a deep breath and said, "You know, you're right. Let him rot in jail. I'm through with this scum. I've heard just about every wisecrack imaginable from your type. Let me tell you, Mr. Emery, I've put so many know-it-alls like you in prison, and I'm going to add you to the list. So you get your attorney and see if you can beat this rap."

Emery clapped his hands. "Are you done now? You ought to try out for a part in a movie about an overzealous cop with a huge ego who goes crazy because he doesn't have enough evidence to convict an innocent man. You'd be perfect for the part." He smiled arrogantly at Munson's red face. "I have other things to do than talk to you. If you're going to charge me, then do it and let me talk to my attorney. If not, let me go because I have a very busy schedule today."

"I'm not done with you yet. Where were you Tuesday afternoon at four o'clock?"

"Four o'clock? At my fitness center. You can check it out. It's at the corner of Vine and Twelfth. I was there from 3:30 until about 6:00. You have to sign in when you enter and sign out when you go. The attendant will verify I was there. He's given me personal training sessions before, so he knows me."

Munson called down to dispatch an officer to the gym, turned back to his suspect, and said, "I can't wait to take you to trial, Mr. Emery. You're going to prison for a long time. You'll wait here while we check out your alibi." He stomped out in disgust.

Ramsey said, "Listen, Emery, you don't know my partner; he could snap at any time. You might not want to mess with him anymore. Tell you what, you can just deal with me from now on. If you sign a confession we'll see to it that you get a deal, two to five years if you turn state's against Bridget. Then you won't have to deal with Munson again."

Emery laughed, "Are you kidding me? That's the worst acting job I've ever seen. After twenty years you'd think you two could put on a better good cop-bad cop routine than that. You can't be serious. You have nothing on me. Either charge me or let me go."

Ramsey shook his head. "Have it your way. I'll see you in court." He left to find Munson, taking Cane with him.

As the three were talking in the corridor, the duty officers reported back in. "Both alibis check out," one officer told them. "The guy at the gym said Emery was there. The usher at the movie also remembered Bridget. In fact, the usher said she was the kind of person who wasn't easy to forget."

Munson said under his breath, "Tell me about it."

The officer said, "There is one thing, though: both the gym attendant and the usher said they could have easily left at any time and come back. All they know is that they were there at the beginning of the movie and the workout, and at the end."

"Thanks," Munson sighed. "I guess we have to turn them loose for now. To convict them on just the testimony of Slaggert would be tough. I'm going to get them, though, wait and see. Cocky people like those two always get overconfident and make mistakes. When they do, I'll be there to pounce on them."

After Bridget and Emery had been released, Ramsey said, "Dennis, I've never seen you like this. Are you all right?"

"I'm fine. It's just — twenty years of punks like Emery has gotten to me. I should be at my son's soccer game and instead I'm dealing with a worthless piece of trash like him. I'm going to get him if it is the last thing I do, and when this is all over I'm going to take a vacation. I need one."

"I hear you," said Cane. "We all need a vacation."

CHAPTER 11

The next morning, Cane overslept and headed into work half an hour late. The ever-punctual investigator had suddenly become the tardy employee. He fumbled around his office for a while and thought about Lindsey. He had had a great time with her before his trip, and had been thinking about her almost constantly since their date.

He decided to go to Lindsey's office and ask her out again. As he headed for the door, a brilliant idea came into his mind. *Yes! That would be perfect. I could get back at Livingston and everyone else at the same time. It seems a little farfetched, but it just might work.*

He was suddenly filled with hope for the future. Before he had reached his breaking point, he would have never considered doing anything so bold. A smile broke out on his face. *You know what? I'm going to do it. What do I have to lose?*

At Lindsey's desk, he said, "Hi Lindsey. I wanted to tell you that I had a great time last Thursday."

"So did I. I thought maybe you didn't, though, because I hadn't heard from you since then."

Cane replied, "Well, you know I was out of town, and yesterday I had a huge break in my case and didn't have time to call. Would you like to go out tonight? I know a really unique bar called The Purple Parrot where we could get a meal. They have live entertainment. Tonight is open mic night and it can be really funny at times, though the crowd can get a little rough on the performers."

"I'd love to go. It sounds like it would be a lot of fun."

"I'll pick you up at seven," said Cane, and headed back to his office. His phone rang just as he got inside.

It was Detective Munson and he had news. "Rachelle was released from the hospital this morning and Curt was right by her side. He spent the entire time she was in the hospital there with her. Are you sure he's using her? He seems to be sincere."

"I don't know," Cane said. "I can think of five million reasons why he'd be putting on an act. I'm sure he still has that weird rocker girl on the side."

"Maybe he thinks he's her 'knight in shining armor' and really likes her. Or maybe he does just want the money and is going to dump her once he gets it."

"No telling with these people. This is one of the strangest cases I've ever seen. Every time I turn around someone else is trying to cheat on someone while using another person. None of these people has a conscience."

"Yeah. Well, Rachelle is apparently going to make a full recovery. I'll give her police protection for a few more days just to be safe. Then I'll have to cut the officer loose; we can't afford that many man hours for one person."

Cane said, "I understand."

"We're not going to press charges against Curt for firing that weapon in public. He was protecting himself and the prosecutor says since we don't have enough evidence yet to convict Emery and Bridget, it wouldn't look good if we charged Curt. That smart-aleck Emery is guilty, and I'm going to prove it."

"Well, keep digging and you'll get him," Cane said. "I've got to go now. I have work to do. I'll catch you later."

He spent the rest of the day writing a report and catching up on office work. All day he thought of Lindsey and how he couldn't wait to see her. The day dragged on until it was finally time to pick her up.

When Lindsey came down to meet him, she said, "I hope this is all right. I dressed semi-casual because the way you described the place we're going, it sounds kind of like a dive."

"You look great. You don't need to be dressed up. Not that I think you aren't dressed up. I just mean that—" he hesitated.

"I know what you mean, and it's okay."

They drove to The Purple Parrot and were given a table six rows back from the stage. After the meal, as they were enjoying their second round of drinks, the announcer came onstage. "As you know, it's open mic night and again we have a packed house. I'm not going to waste any of your time so our first act is Julie Jones, singer extraordinaire. Let's give her a warm welcome."

The crowd was silent as a heavyset woman came onstage and began to sing to prerecorded background music. She was horrible; the crowd didn't take long to respond, throwing plastic beer bottles at her as they had at Angel. After a minute or so of abusive comments and bottles flying her way, the woman gave up and left the stage.

The waitress returned to Cane and Lindsey's table and Lindsey ordered two more drinks. Cane said, "Wow, I haven't even finished my second one."

Lindsey said, "That's okay, you can catch up later."

The announcer returned and said, "Now welcome one of our regulars, comedian Sam Jam."

Sam Jam came on and the crowd booed loudly. Sam Jam said, "What do you call a short psychic who breaks out of jail? A small medium at large." The crowd quieted and a few people actually laughed. Sam Jam continued with, "What do you call a blonde with half a brain? Gifted." The crowd laughed a little more.

He went on, "A cop pulled over a dumb guy and said, 'Your eyes are red. Have you been drinking?' The dumb guy answered, 'Your eyes look glazed, officer. Have you been at the donut shop?'" Now the crowd groaned and began to boo.

Sam Jam raised his voice to make himself heard and continued, "Did you hear there's a new restaurant on the moon? It has great food, but no atmosphere." Ten or fifteen plastic bottles went flying up towards the stage and hit the protective fence as the crowd booed wildly.

The announcer hastened back onstage and called, "You're out of here!" Sam Jam shuffled off stage shouting profanities at the audience, and the announcer cut in, "Give a big round of applause for Billy Barnes, country singer."

An ugly man walked up on stage dressed in blue jeans, T-shirt, cowboy hat and boots. He struck a chord on his folk guitar and began to sing, and suddenly the mood in the room changed. He sounded great. The crowd began to cheer him on and not a single bottle was thrown. When he was done, the crowd clapped and yelled in approval.

The next performer was announced as Brad Jefferies, who came on stage and began to sing. After a few seconds, when the crowd realized how terrible he was, they began to throw bottles as usual.

Lindsey turned to Cane and said, "This beer has really hit me. Do you mind if I throw a bottle at the fence?"

Cane looked at her, surprised, and said, "Go ahead."

She took a beer bottle from their table and chucked it at the stage. She began to laugh and then to boo loudly. Cane looked at Lindsey in surprise; then, impulsively, he too picked up a bottle and hurled it at the fence. He laughed and yelled, "Get him off the stage."

"This is fun," cried Lindsey over the commotion.

"Yeah, it is," said Cane. They picked up another pair of bottles and hurled them in unison, laughing. They spent the rest of the evening laughing and having a great time.

When Cane finally got Lindsey home, she enthusiastically kissed him good night and told him she'd see him in the morning at work. He drove home feeling good about his life and about himself. Lying in bed, he looked back on his life; he couldn't believe he had taken forty-one years to realize that there was more to life than work; he couldn't believe how much he'd missed out on. His last thought before falling asleep was: *I'm so glad I changed, and I'm so glad I asked Lindsey out.*

$$ \$ \$ \$ $$

The next morning Cane woke up feeling groggy and a little hung over. He pulled himself together, had a cup of coffee and a Motrin, and went off to work. Despite feeling ill physically, he smiled all the way to work remembering how much fun he'd had the night before.

After sitting at his desk for a while, he started to feel much better. He was startled by the sound of his phone ringing. He answered it and heard Munson's voice. "Cane?"

"Yeah? What's up?"

"Rachelle Johnson is back in the hospital, fighting for her life. Apparently she overdosed on drugs. I don't know the details yet. You'd better get over to the hospital. I'll meet you there."

"I'll be there as soon as I can."

As he hurried to the hospital, Cane's cheeriness turned to concern. Even though he didn't particularly care for Rachelle, he didn't want to see Bridget get any of the settlement if he could help it. He also felt a little sorry for Rachelle now, because after all, she had been shot and could have died.

When Cane arrived at the hospital, Munson was already questioning Curt. As he walked up, he heard Munson say, "So let me get this straight. You didn't know how many of those pills she was taking?"

"No. I had no idea," Curt said. "The bottle said to take one for pain every six hours. I didn't think to monitor what she took. She was in such terrible pain that she probably just kept taking them thinking it would eventually work."

"So you let her take enough to make her pass out?"

"Now wait a minute. I didn't let her do anything. She's an adult and I never had any idea she would do this."

"Let's see, there are eight left in the bottle," Munson said. "That means that she must have taken twelve in a ten-hour period. Are you crazy? It's a wonder she isn't dead already."

Curt fought back. "She only took four all day. She must have gotten up in the middle of the night and taken the other eight. You should be thanking me; if I hadn't come into the bathroom and seen her lying on the floor, she probably would've been dead by morning. When I tried to wake her she didn't respond so I called for help and we ended up back here again."

"We let you slide on the weapons charges because no one got hurt. If she dies, there'll be a full investigation and you may be facing charges."

"Give me a break," said Curt. "I didn't do anything wrong. It's your fault she's here in the first place. If you'd given her police protection after that first attempt on her life, this wouldn't have happened."

"Don't blame all this on me. I didn't monitor her prescription."

"Can't you just leave me alone?" Curt pleaded. "I . . . I don't know what I would do without her. I . . . I think I love her."

"If you loved her, you wouldn't let her take twelve pills and overdose, now would you?"

Curt didn't say anything.

Cane butted in with, "She has to make it. She just has to."

Curt and Munson stared at Cane in bafflement.

"Why do you care so much if she lives?" Curt said. "I thought all you cared about was saving your company money. The longer you have to wait to pay out, the better, right? If there's an attempted murder charge pending against Bridget and your main beneficiary dies, you could hold up the payout until the trial. I know you don't really care about Rachelle."

"I don't want to see anyone die," said Cane nervously. "I just hope she makes it."

"Cane, I've known you for twenty years," said Munson. "You seem different. What's going on? Are you all right?"

"I'm fine. Can't I just want someone to be all right?"

"Yeah, I guess so." Munson turned to Curt. "You should know, Curt, we didn't charge Bridget and her boyfriend yet. They have almost flawless alibis and we can't get a conviction on Slaggert's testimony alone."

Curt's face turned red. "You mean to tell me those guys get to hire someone to kill Rachelle and me and they're going to get off scot-free? On top of that, if Rachelle dies, that degenerate is going to get a good chunk of insurance money that she doesn't deserve."

"Not necessarily. The investigation isn't over by any means. Let's not speculate until we find out if Rachelle is going to pull through. Then we can talk about our options."

After about fifteen minutes, the emergency room doctor came out and introduced himself to Curt as Dr. Madison.

Curt immediately asked, "How is she?"

"It's too soon to tell. We pumped her stomach, but unfortunately a large portion of the medication had digested already. Her blood pressure is very low and she's not out of the woods yet. We should know something within the next six hours."

"Doctor, she has to make it," Cane exclaimed. "Do everything you can!"

"We're doing everything we can," said Dr. Madison, "and we'll know more soon. I'm sorry, but I have to go now. I have more patients in need of assistance and we're understaffed as usual. I'll be back the moment we have an update."

Munson drew Cane aside for a private conversation and abruptly said, "What's going on, Wendell? You've never been this wrapped up in a case before. Do you have a vested interest here?"

"No, Dennis, I don't. I don't know what's gotten into me. I'm just pulling for her and I don't know why. Maybe it's because I dislike Bridget so much, or I could just be feeling sorry for Rachelle. And besides, I'm burned out. I want this nightmare of a case to end. You of all people should know what that's like. Every time I turn around something else happens, and I haven't been able to prove one iota of fraud yet. Sometimes I think I'd be better off just giving up on this case and starting over with the next one."

"That's not like you to give up so easily. You usually fight tooth and nail until you get the job done. I mean, you hate losing a case more than I do."

"I don't like losing a case, it's true, but the fact is that Bridget may just get off on the conspiracy charge and end up with the money. How right is that?"

"It isn't. Let's just wait and hope for the best."

Cane brightened and said, "You know what? You're right. I'm going to do everything in my power to stop Bridget from ever getting a penny of that money."

"Now that's the Cane I remember. I have to go back to the station now; I'll meet you back here at five o'clock." The two investigators went their separate ways.

Back at Cane's office, he found a message on his answering machine: *"Cane, I need to see you right away about the Rankin case. As soon as you get this message come up to my office."* It was from Chad Livingston.

Suddenly Cane felt hopeless. *You know what?* Cane thought, *I'm not going up there today. I don't care what that idiot does to me; I'm going to avoid him altogether. I'll just say I was at the hospital and didn't get his message.*

He spent the rest of the afternoon preparing documents for claims to be settled, then headed over to the hospital at five o'clock as Munson had asked him to do. He arrived to find Curt standing in a corridor with Angel.

They didn't see him, so he stood patiently eavesdropping around the corner. He heard Angel saying, "That's it, Curt. Either you love me or you don't."

"You know I love you, but what am I supposed to do?" Curt pleaded. "She overdosed and almost died a second time. I have to be here when she wakes up. Do you want to blow it for us?"

"I don't care anymore about the money or a singing career. You have to make a choice right now. Is it going to be her, or me?" Angel said.

"Come on, babe, don't do this. You know how I feel about you."

"You heard me. Make a choice. It's either her or me."

"I can't leave her right now. What if she dies? I just can't do it."

Angel yelled, "Fine! Your choice is made. Remember, you were the one who made it." In tears, she ran around the corner, past Cane without seeing him. Curt followed, calling, "Come on, babe. Don't do this. Come back!"

"Just leave me alone," sobbed Angel, and she made for the exit.

Curt noticed Cane and realized he had been listening. "What are you looking at?"

Cane said, "Don't worry. I knew about you and her my first day on this case. I actually saw her sing at The Purple Parrot." Curt's face darkened. "Don't worry," Cane went on, "I'm not going to say anything. I may be cold and heartless, but I'm not going to get in the middle of Angel and Rachelle. That's for you to work out on your own."

Curt looked at Cane as if seeing him in a new light. Cane surmised that Curt probably wanted someone to talk to after all he'd been through in the last couple of days. Cane was never good at being supportive or sensitive, so he tried to strike up a conversation the best way he knew. "So your goal is to see Angel become a star one day? She's cute, but what do you think?"

"Are you kidding me?" Curt said. "She couldn't sing if her life depended on it and I know that. I just tell her she can because that's all she has. She's young and she really doesn't have anything else going for her. She needs me, but Rachelle needs me too. I don't know what to do. I mean, I love Angel, but I think I love Rachelle, too."

Cane replied, "I don't know what you should do, but I do know you shouldn't be stringing along two women at the same time. Eventually you're going to get caught. Rachelle seems to be the kind of person who wouldn't take it well. If she found out you crossed her, I don't know what she'd do. She seems like the vengeful type."

Suddenly Curt remembered to whom he was talking and said, "Back off, Jack! It's none of your business how many women I see. What are you doing snooping around here anyway, when Rachelle is fighting for her life?"

"Like I said before, I'm not going to say anything about Angel. You have enough to worry about. Believe it or not, I'm actually pulling for Rachelle. I don't know about you, but I can't stand Bridget. Man, she's a nasty person! Besides, I have to see if Rachelle is the one who'll be receiving our check."

That statement about the check pleased Curt and he said, "I guess it's okay if you stay. I just hope she'll be all right." Cane nodded as a nurse walked up.

The nurse said, "I have good news, Mr. Clark. It looks like Miss Johnson's condition is improving. Her blood pressure has stabilized and she's coming around now. She's very lucky to be alive, for the second time this week. I wouldn't push your luck a third time."

Curt yelled, "Yes! Thank you, God!" Cane sighed in relief as well.

The nurse continued, "You can't see her until tomorrow, so I suggest you go get some sleep tonight and come back in the morning. She's in good hands. We have the finest doctors here at County and we'll notify you if we need you." The nurse smiled and walked away.

Cane said, "Well, that's good news."

"Yeah," Curt added. "what a relief."

Cane hesitated, thinking of the one cardinal rule he had as an investigator. He never, under any circumstances, would ever associate with a person on a case he was investigating. He knew if he did get involved with a client, his judgment could be clouded and he could end up in trouble if he didn't make rational decisions about the case.

A new thought entered his mind: *You know what? I don't care about the old rational Cane. I'm a new man and this guy could use a friend right now. I'm going to help if I can.*

So he said, "Hey Curt. Do you want to go get a beer or something?"

Startled, Curt hesitated for a moment. *He might just be trying to get more information from me. Then again, he already knows about Angel and me, so what could he possibly gain? If I get close to him, maybe I can persuade him to turn the check over sooner. I don't see any harm in it.*

He said aloud, "Sure. Why not? There's a pub called Manny's about half a mile away, on Washington Boulevard."

"I know where that is," Cane said.

"Okay, I'll meet you there in a few minutes."

Cane called Munson on the way to the bar. "Why didn't you meet me at the hospital?"

"I got tied up at the station. I have other cases besides this one, you know. My kid has a soccer game tonight and my wife will kill me if I don't make it. She gave me an ultimatum: either go to his game tonight or sleep on the couch. I hate sleeping on the couch. Besides, she's put up with too much from me lately. She says I'm never home, and she's right."

"Relax, Dennis. You need to stop burning the candle at both ends. Go to the soccer game tonight and don't worry about your job. It'll be waiting for you in the morning."

"Are you sure this is Cane I'm talking to? Mr. Stay Out All Night to Stake Out a Suspect? You're right, though. I need some time off. This job is really getting to me."

Yeah, it used to get to me too, but not anymore, Cane thought. Aloud he added, "Oh, by the way . . . Rachelle is going to make it. She should be much better by tomorrow."

"That's good news. Listen, I have to go if I'm ever going to get out of here today. I'll talk to you tomorrow." Munson hung up and Cane pulled up and entered the bar, which was a dive, reeking of stale beer and old cigarette butts. It held fifteen tables and some stools lined up along an old wooden bar. Cane spotted Curt already sitting at a table and went to join him.

A middle-aged, heavyset waitress walked up and said, "What'll you have?"

Cane said, "I'll just have a Coke."

"If you aren't having a beer, then why did you ask me to come here?"

"I guess there's no reason why I can't have one. Okay, I'll have a Pabst Blue Ribbon."

Curt laughed. "I haven't had a Pabst in years."

A little embarrassed, Cane said, "Fine, I'll take whatever you're having."

The waitress said, "Two Bud Lights, coming right up."

After the waitress left, Curt said, "So what's on your mind, Cane? I'm sure you didn't invite me here to socialize and make a new friend."

Cane began to speak as the waitress brought the beers and put them on the table. "I'm really sorry about Rachelle. I'm glad she made it."

Cane paid the waitress and then Curt, wallowing in his misery, replied, "Yeah, why do you care? I heard you're a cold-hearted snake who only cares about the company that you work for."

Cane took a sip of his beer and countered with, "I guess I used to be, but not anymore. The company couldn't care less about you or me. I guess when you get a little older you start seeing what's really important in life and you change a little."

"Boy, you're a tough one to figure out," said Curt. "At times you seem like a self-centered idiot and other times you seem almost human."

They each took a long drink from their bottles and Cane mused, "I hope Bridget doesn't come after her again. It would be a shame to see her get that money."

Curt fired back, "Well, if she does, this time I'll be ready." Then it sank in that Cane was finally talking about paying out. This brought a smile to Curt's face and he asked, "Well, when are you going to pay us?"

Cane was starting to feel a little tingle from the beer and said, "I don't know. I just don't know." He sipped his beer again. "You don't mind if I ask you a personal question, do you?"

"Go ahead."

"How long are you going to string those two women on? Because I hope this case will be over soon so I don't have to see it blow up in your face."

Normally Curt would have told off anyone who spoke so personally to him or delved into his private life as Cane had. This time though, he remembered that it behooved him to stay on Cane's good side. He said, "I don't know what I'm going to do. You know, I really do love them both in their own different ways. I guess it doesn't matter, though, because the way it looks, it's over with Angel anyway." A thought dawned on him. "So that's why you invited me out for a drink. You want to blackmail me for part of that insurance settlement so you won't tell Rachelle about Angel. That's what you meant by it blowing up in my face. Well, I don't care if she finds out. I think I love Rachelle and it's probably over with Angel anyway."

"No, no, you took what I said all wrong. I would never blackmail you."

Curt stood up, frowning. "I don't care what you meant. All I know is that you're going to pay up soon. If you cross me, let's just say you won't have to worry about anything but who the beneficiary is on your own insurance policy, if you know what I mean."

"Back off! I didn't mean it that way," Cane said.

Curt got right up in Cane's face and said, "I don't care how you meant it! Stay out of my business. If you make so much as a peep to Rachelle about Angel I'm going to come looking for you." Curt stalked to the door, snarling over his shoulder, "You better get that check ready, because we aren't going to wait much longer. That's a promise."

Cane had been threatened many times before and never took it as more than idle threats. Now he sat and thought, *I'm going to do it. I'm going to do what I thought up the other day. I don't care about the consequences. These people are driv-*

ing me crazy and I don't care about any of them. That's what I get for trying to be nice and trying to help Curt. I get threatened. I'm going to do it.

He stood up, tossed a tip on the table, and left the bar feeling like a man on a mission. *I've been in the business twenty years and I'm not letting some big-mouth like Curt intimidate me. I'll show him.* He drove back to his apartment and began making his plans. His future looked bright now. Cane went to sleep that night with dreams of taking his Philadelphia Mutual termination settlement and retiring.

CHAPTER 12

ane woke up feeling refreshed and drove to work filled with positive thoughts about his future. He was fiddling around his office when his phone rang; it was Munson. "Cane, I spoke to the hospital and they're releasing Rachelle today. I'm leaving the guard on her for another two days. I hope this time she takes care of herself. Man, she's messed up. I get the feeling she'll never be happy."

"I get the feeling she's going to end up back in the hospital again, or worse." Just then Cane's other line rang and he said, "Munson, I have another call. I have to go."

"All right. I'll keep you posted if I get any new breaks on the case."

Cane quickly switched lines. "Wendell Cane speaking. Can I help you?"

"Yes, you can help me," Livingston said. "You can get up to my office right away."

"I'll be right up, sir." On the way upstairs, he thought, *I was just starting to feel good about myself and was ready to have a great day. Now it has to be ruined by talking to that clown. I'm just going to tell him what he wants to hear and then do what I want. After all, he's letting me go for no good reason as soon as I'm done with this case.*

Livingston was champing at the bit. "Where have you been? I asked to see you yesterday about the Rankin case."

"I'm sorry, sir, but as you know, an attempt was made on Rachelle Johnson's life. Yesterday she went back to the hospital with an overdose of her pain medication."

"Is she all right?" Livingston asked.

"Yes, it looks like she'll be fine. She almost died, though. The doctor said that if they'd waited two hours longer, she wouldn't have made it."

Livingston frowned. "That's unfortunate. If she hadn't lived, we could have easily postponed the payout at least another sixty days."

Cane took a deep breath. "Sir, with all due respect, this is a young woman's life we're talking about. She almost died. Aren't you being a little insensitive?"

"Insensitive? Oh come on, Cane. You know how it is in this business. Besides, I read your report and it appears she was just along for the ride with Jim Rankin. She really doesn't deserve the money."

"It's true that she doesn't deserve the money," said Cane, "but she's the beneficiary on the policy. It isn't our place to judge her motives if indeed there was no fraud."

Livingston did a double-take. "What's gotten into you? I've never seen you like this. Have you been watching too much TV? This is the real world here, with real consequences to real stockholders when we have to pay a claim like that. Don't tell me you've gone soft on me."

Cane didn't say anything for a moment as his thoughts boiled inside him. *What a jerk. I can't believe I went along with this guy all these years. What made me sacrifice my integrity to work for him? Why did I take so long to realize I have to do what's right? I can't win with this idiot. I'm just going to go along with him so I can leave the company with what little self-respect I have.*

He heard Livingston repeating, "Did you hear me, Cane? Have you gone soft on me?"

"No, of course not, sir."

"Then go out and find a reason not to pay this claim, and if you can't do that, at least get me another sixty-day extension. Now go and leave me alone, but keep me posted about this case. You know I have golf today so don't disturb me unless it's important."

Cane merely said, "Yes, sir." He walked calmly out of the office, but he was furious with Livingston for being such an idiot and furious with himself for going along with him for so long. He went back to his office and brooded. *I'm going to do something nice for someone. I'm going to send Lindsey flowers. After all, she's the only person in this place I truly care about.* He found a florist in the phone book and arranged for flowers to be delivered that afternoon, with a card:

Dear Lindsey,

Thank you for being a great friend and a great person. You've made me realize what is truly important in life, and I don't know how I'll ever repay you for that.

Thanks again,
Wendell

Later that afternoon, Cane headed back to Livingston's office as Livingston was getting ready to practice his putting. He looked up and saw Cane and said, "This had better be good if you're interrupting my practice again. My game is in the dumper. I'm slicing the ball off the tee and I can't putt for squat. Now what is it this time?"

Cane said, "I'm sorry, sir, but I have some bad news."

"About which case?"

"Not about a case. Remember the cousin I went to visit a week ago? Well, he died."

"I thought it was your second cousin."

Cane hesitated and said, "Uh, it is my second cousin. I just call him my cousin. It's kind of like calling your wife your spouse."

"Don't remind me of my wife!" Livingston said. "You're not married, are you? Well, you're lucky. My wife has made my life miserable for the last ten years. That woman is never happy, I swear."

She's never happy because you haven't been a good husband, Cane thought. *When you're married, you're supposed to put top priority on your marriage and if you cared about anyone besides yourself, you'd have had a great marriage.*

"My advice to you, Cane, is never get married in the first place. Save yourself the aggravation. Anyway, what does your second cousin have to do with me? I didn't even know him."

Cane said, "Well, I'm going to need Friday off for the funeral."

"Are you kidding me? You need another day off right in the middle of this huge case? Can't you just send a nice card and flowers like I always do? I hate funerals, and flowers always seem to do the trick."

"I can't. I have to go to the funeral."

"Well, I don't like it at all, but I suppose I have to say yes."

"Thank you, sir."

"Now leave me alone and let me get my practice in before my game."

"One more thing," Cane said. "I need you to sign these forms so I can get caught up before I leave."

Livingston grabbed a pen and the folders, glaring at Cane as he signed the claims without reading them. "Now let me get back to my putting." Cane just nodded and left the room.

Back in his office, he called his travel agent and explained that he needed a flight out the next morning. It was crucial that it departed as early as possible, and that it returned late on Sunday.

When Cane hung up the phone, he felt invigorated. He had never traveled twice in one month before. He went to see if Lindsey had received her flowers, and to tell her he was going out of town again.

When Lindsey saw him, she looked around to make sure no one was looking, and stood up to hug Cane. "Thank you for the flowers. That card was one of the nicest things anyone ever said to me. You really made me feel special."

Cane blushed a little. "Well, I meant every word of it. You are special. Since we went out that day, I've been thinking a lot about you."

Now Lindsey blushed as well. "Yeah, me too."

Cane said, "I have to go out of town again until late Sunday. I just wanted to let you know I wasn't avoiding you."

"I hope everything is all right," Lindsey replied.

"It's just I have something I have to do."

"I'll see you when you get back, right?"

"Of course you will." He handed her a few files and said, "Will you make sure these get paid right away?"

"Sure thing, Mr. Cane."

He grinned; he loved it when she called him Mr. Cane. "Thanks. And I will definitely see you when I get back."

Back in his office, he called and left Munson a message saying that he would be gone for a few days.

$$\$ \; \$ \; \$$

Meanwhile, Bridget and Rick Emery met at a park to discuss their options. Emery said, "We can't afford to take any more chances like that! She's under police protection now and impossible to get to. I can't believe those guys missed like that. They were supposed to be good. They were nothing but amateurs."

Bridget added, "Yeah, well, they can't leave a cop with her forever. I just hope they take the protection away before they pay her off, or we're done. I thought we'd gotten lucky when she overdosed. No matter how, though, I'm not going to let her get her hands on my money. We'd better figure out something quickly because who knows when that freak Cane is going to release the check. Do you think that snitch's testimony will be enough to convict us?"

"Are you kidding me?" said Emery. "If that under-achieving detective had a case he would've charged us. That guy's so stupid he probably needs his partner to tie his shoes for him. What we have to do is find a way to get close to Rachelle again. It's not going to be so easy to get solid alibis like last time. I need time to come up with something, and time is the one thing we don't have. Let me do some think-ing. If anything happens, let me know."

$ $ $

About an hour later, Curt went to the hospital to pick up Rachelle and take her home. He asked, "How are you feeling, baby?"

Rachelle, surprised by his new tenderness, said, "I feel a little woozy, but otherwise okay."

"Well, don't ever do that to me again. I was worried sick about you. I did a lot of thinking while you were in here and I don't know what I'd do if you were gone."

She looked up at Curt and saw a look of true concern in his eyes. For the first time, she wondered if she might be falling for Curt.

$ $ $

After returning home late Sunday night, Cane got up bright and early Monday and went down to the police sta-tion to see Munson. Crosby was waiting for him at the front desk. "Well, look at what the cat dragged in. It's a slimy snake named Cane."

Cane snapped back, "Don't you have any respect? I don't deserve that remark! I have feelings just like everyone else. Every time I come here you put me down and I'm not taking it anymore!"

"Wow! What happened to you?" Crosby said. "I'm sorry if you're in a bad mood. I won't joke with you anymore."

Cane laughed. "Man, are you ever gullible, and did I ever have you going! I've seen earthworms with more brains than you. I can't believe you fell for that. I win this one."

"You had me going for a minute, but only because you're so unpredictable and I think you could actually snap at any time. I'm going to get you back for that one."

"Fine, fine. Is Munson in?"

"He's here. Go on back."

"You're such a one-upper, Crosby. You always try to outdo me. You're such a last-worder too. You always have to try and get the last word in when we talk."

"I do not."

Cane walked through the security door and just before it closed he said, "You do too," so Crosby wouldn't have a chance to respond. Cane laughed and walked toward Munson's office and, about three seconds later, over the P.A., Crosby said, "I do not." Cane laughed again and looked around for Munson.

After he found Munson he asked, "Anything new on the conspiracy charge against Bridget?"

"No. We have the shooter dead to rights, but nothing new on her and Emery. It looks like they might walk. I'm not giving up yet, though."

Cane felt disappointed. "I was afraid of that. I have nothing, either."

Munson said, "Rachelle went home from the hospital Friday and it was quiet over there all weekend, so I had to pull the protection. I had no choice."

"I know. Oh well. I was more or less just checking in. I'm headed to the office and I'll catch up with you later."

When he arrived in his office, there was a note from Livingston saying he wanted to see him in his office immediately. He went up to the office and Livingston said, "Cane, I know what you're doing and I won't have any part of it."

All of a sudden Cane had a nervous feeling in his stomach and his knees felt weak. He said, "What do you mean, sir?"

"I know you haven't taken a day off in seven years and I realize you're just trying to use your vacation days so you don't have to give them back. Every year before this one you gave your vacation days back and you don't have any family so I'm not going to approve any more days off this year for you unless it's an emergency."

Cane felt momentarily relieved that Livingston was talking about his vacation days, but then thought: *Are you kidding me? This guy's so cheap he doesn't want me to take my vacation days before he lets me go, and he'll get millions when he leaves. He's a bigger jerk than I thought. I just have to hold on a little while longer and then I won't have to ever deal with him again.*

He regained his composure and said, "Oh no, sir. I wouldn't do that. I won't be taking any more time off."

Livingston replied, "All right then. You can go now."

Cane left the room, took a deep breath in relief, and went back to his office. He spent the rest of the day brooding over his disgust for Livingston and the unfairness of it all.

The next morning was spent planning what he was going to do when Livingston let him go. He was supposed to meet Lindsey for lunch, and about an hour before their date the phone rang. It was Lindsey and she was clearly upset.

"Wendell, they finally did it."

"Did what?"

"They let me go! I got my pink slip today. They laid me off." Lindsey started sniffling a little and said, "What am I going to do?"

"You'll be fine," Cane said. "Trust me. Meet me at that café for lunch in an hour just like we planned." Lindsey agreed and hung up.

When Cane arrived at the café, Lindsey was already there. She was sitting at a table off to the side and looked like she'd been crying.

He approached her gently and said, "Are you all right?"

"No, I'm not all right. I put in fifteen years at that company and they treated me like a common criminal. My supervisor, Bill, and two security guards approached me without warning. Bill handed me an envelope with a letter from the company president saying that, due to unfortunate financial circumstances, Philadelphia Mutual would not be requiring my employment anymore.

"After that he said, 'You're going to have to pack up your things now and security will escort you out of the building. And do you know, they stood there and watched every move I made, and escorted me all the way to my car. That's when I called you."

"Don't worry," said Cane. "Between your severance and mine, we'll be fine. I'm sure the axe is going to come down on me next. Did you do everything I told you to do?"

"Yes I did, just in the nick of time," Lindsey said.

"Good. I'm going to try to hold on there as long as I can. Livingston won't do anything if the case with Rachelle is still ongoing. If I can just make it three more days until Friday, I'll be all right."

Lindsey said, "Wendell, I—" She hesitated and went on, "Well, I just wanted to thank you for being such a good friend. My life has been so much better since you and I have been going out."

"Listen," said Cane, "since I met you, my life has changed so much. I realize now what's important in life. I just wish I had asked you out years ago." He took her hand and said, "Now, I want you to go home and try not to worry. Everything is going to be all right."

$ $ $

Cane finished out the week at work just as he'd hoped. On Friday morning, he was in his office when his phone rang. Livingston barked, "Cane, I want you up in my office immediately!" and hung up on him. Cane felt sick to his stomach as he walked up to Livingston's office. *Is this it? Am I being let go?*

When he entered the office, Livingston shouted, "Cane! What's wrong with you?" Cane saw Bentley, the vice-president of Philadelphia Mutual, and two security guards standing off to the side. Livingston looked livid.

Cane suddenly thought of Lindsey and felt at ease. Whatever happened next, it didn't matter, because he had a true friend he could count on now. He couldn't change what Livingston was going to do, but he could change his future and have a great relationship with a tremendous woman.

"Did you hear me?" Livingston yelled. "What's wrong with you? You sent through that five million dollar payout without my approval! You knew I wanted to get a continuance on the investigation and hold off on the payout. Why did you do that?"

Cane smiled widely. "You did approve it, sir. You know a payout that size couldn't go through without your signature."

Livingston protested, "You must have forged my signature — I never would have signed that!"

"On the contrary, sir, you did sign it."

"I did not. I never even saw the final report."

Cane walked over to Livingston's desk and said, "Oh yes, you saw it. It's right here on your desk." He picked up a stack of files and pulled out the one on the bottom of the pile.

Livingston grabbed the file out of Cane's hand, looked at it a moment, and said, "You buried that file on my desk so I wouldn't see it."

"Now why would I do that? I have nothing to gain from this payout."

Livingston growled, "Well, you still forged my signature. I'll bring you up on charges."

Cane was ready for him. "I didn't forge your signature. Remember that day I came in when you were too busy to be bothered because of your golf game? You said you could-n't be disturbed because you'd been slicing the ball so much and your putting was atrocious. Well, you grabbed the file and signed it and told me not to disturb you again. I tried to talk to you but you shooed me out of your office so fast that I couldn't."

Livingston gnashed his teeth, clenched his fist, pound-ed on his desk hard and cried, "Cane! How could you do this after all I've done for you?"

Cane thought of Lindsey again and remained calm. "All you've done for me? You mean all I've done for you. I've spent twenty years here, taking your garbage and still say-ing, 'Yes sir, no sir.' I was your top investigator and I saved this company millions. What *you* have done for *me*? Please!"

Livingston turned to Bentley and said, "I want a stop payment put on that check immediately."

Bentley said, "We can't do it, sir. The check cleared two days ago."

Livingston yelled, "Who in Accounts Payable is respon-sible for this? I want them in here immediately."

Bentley said, "I already checked on that, sir. An employee by the name of Lindsey Washington sent it through." A tremendous feeling of victory came over Cane. He felt like he had just gotten revenge for every little man who had ever been pushed around by his boss. He felt like someone in the world had finally stood up to the people on top who always look down on the workers.

Livingston said, "Send for her right now."

Bentley replied, "I'm afraid it's not possible, sir. We laid her off a few days ago. Her severance has been paid out already, as well."

Livingston groaned and said, "Well, there has to be someone we can hold accountable for this." He looked around. Both security guards, Bentley, and Cane looked at Livingston with raised eyebrows as if to say *Yes, you're to blame.* Livingston bit his lip and said, "You haven't heard the last of this, Cane!"

"Oh really? I think I have," Cane said. "You see, Rachelle Johnson had the money coming to her and it's an open and shut case. You would've had to pay her eventually. You're the one who signed off on it. I did nothing wrong."

All eyes in the room were on Livingston. Wanting to reassert his authority, he barked, "Well give him his walking papers at least! And we should hold back his severance as well!"

Bentley drew Livingston aside. "Sir, that might not be a good idea. Mr. Cane has been a loyal employee for twenty years and everyone else got severance packages. If we hold back on his, we could have a bigger mess on our hands than we already do. Cane could end up suing us and getting more than just his severance, and you did sign the payout."

Livingston thought for a moment. "Go ahead. Give it to him."

Bentley handed Cane an envelope with a letter in it that said, "Due to unfortunate circumstances that are out of our control, Philadelphia Mutual is sorry to inform you we will no longer be needing your services. A handsome severance package will be provided to you." The document went over all the financial aspects of Cane's separation.

Cane sat there quietly. He had thought he'd take this hard, but he was wrong. He felt relieved that it was all over.

Bentley said, "These are your settlement figures. With your severance, your 401(k), and your retirement, you will be receiving $181,242. The check should be mailed to you next week. We appreciate your long years of service and dedication."

Livingston cut Bentley off and said, "You don't have to go into all that with him after what he did!" Seeing Cane smile serenely, he added bitterly, "Get him out of here."

The security guards approached Cane and motioned for him to leave. Cane stood up and said, "Oh, one more thing, sir. I hope you get that golf swing of yours corrected, because I know how important it is to you. Have a great day."

Livingston turned red. The payout, his lousy marriage, and even the fact that he was a terrible golfer all came to a head. He had hit his breaking point and he yelled, "Get him out of here! All of you get out of here!" He picked up a paperweight and wildly threw it against the wall, knocking a picture to the floor.

Cane was promptly escorted out of the room and to his office, where he packed up all his things while the security guards watched. When he was done, one of the guards said, "I'll be sad to see you go. You were one great investigator."

"Yes I was, wasn't I? I just can't believe I was so stupid all these years and didn't see Livingston for what he really was."

The other guard said, "He's a real scumbag. No one in the company likes him." Cane nodded and allowed himself to be escorted from the building.

As Cane looked back on his former office, he felt no regrets. *This is the first day of the rest of my life, and I'm going to make it great*, he thought as he drove away. Once home, he called Lindsey to let her know he was no longer employed by Philadelphia Mutual. He put his feet up on his coffee table and thought, *I'm glad that's all over with. I feel great!*

$ $ $

Three days later, Cane's severance check came in the mail as promised. He called Lindsey and talked her into going on a long vacation with him in a few days' time.

The morning before they were supposed to leave, Cane got up early to pay Lindsey a visit. As he was walking toward his car, someone grabbed him from behind and wrapped their arm around his neck and shoved his face against the cold metal of the hood of his car. He heard Curt's voice growl, "I ought to kill you right now."

Curt let go of Cane's neck and roughly flipped him over on his back, pinning him against the car. Cane, his heart racing, mustered the courage to gasp, "What's this all about?"

Curt tightened his grip on Cane's shirt and pulled out a switchblade knife with his other hand. "You know what this is about." He pressed a button on the knife and the blade snapped out. Holding the blade to Cane's throat, he demanded, "Where is our five million dollars?"

Cane began to tremble, but managed to say, "What do you mean?"

"We called Philadelphia Mutual and they said the insurance money was paid out a week ago. They said you were the one who approved it." He pinned Cane a little harder. "Now, where's our money?"

Cane gasped to catch his breath. "Loosen up so I can tell you."

Curt loosened up his grip on Cane's shirt ever so slightly. "You have ten seconds to talk or I'm going to start cutting."

Cane said nervously, "Let me explain. Philadelphia Mutual was going to do everything in their power to not pay Rachelle. I overheard the head of the company talking about how he was going to delay the payment indefinitely. I also heard him say he was going to let me go after this case was over. That jerk was going to do a number on both me and Rachelle.

"I got so fed up with Philadelphia Mutual and my boss that I took the claim and pushed it through, even though I wasn't finished with my investigation. Don't you see? If it weren't for me, it would have taken forever for you to get the money, if you ever got it at all. You should be thanking me instead of hurting me. I even ended up losing my job over it. Well, sort of. As I said, the company was going to lay me off and what better excuse to use to terminate me than sneaking your claim through and making sure it was paid?"

"You lost your job because you put our claim through?"

"Well, that was a big part of it. Anyway, I'm no longer with Philadelphia Mutual. I have absolutely nothing to do with them anymore, so I would appreciate it if you left me alone."

Curt said, "Well, where's our money?"

Cane looked at Curt in a puzzled way. "It's in Rachelle's account. You mean to tell me you didn't know?"

Curt let go of him slowly. "Rachelle's account? What account?"

"I don't understand," Cane said. "When Jim Rankin had that policy taken out, he set up an account overseas to put the money in upon his death. It's not that uncommon, really, for someone to do this. That way there's no tax on the interest, and no one can get their hands on the money. Unless your name is on the account you can't touch it. Even our government can't touch it with a court order. That's international banking law. The money was transferred to the offshore account about a week ago. Rachelle should have been notified."

Curt looked a little sick. Cane said, "Oh, no. When was the last time you saw Rachelle?"

Curt hesitated and said, "Two days ago. She said she wasn't feeling well and I haven't been over there since."

"You don't think she played you, do you? That's a lot of money."

Curt said reluctantly, "I don't think she'd do that. We're in love."

Cane laughed. "We're talking about five million dollars here, but if you say you're in love, then I guess you're right."

Curt took a deep breath. "No. She wouldn't do that; she and I are tight."

"You know, technically that money is hers to do as she wants with it. Legally you have no claim to it."

Curt growled, "Shut up, you idiot! No one, and I mean no one double-crosses me. I always get revenge. The first thing I'm going to do is see why I haven't heard from Rachelle in two days. And you'd better be telling me the truth or the next time I come after you, you won't be walking away!"

"Check it out at Philadelphia Mutual," Cane said. "In fact, I know just the person you should talk to. His name is Chad Livingston. He's the one I overheard talking about not paying Rachelle out. You and he would get along really well; you're a lot alike. He's pretty high up in the company, so don't let him give you the runaround."

"Oh, I'll be talking to him for sure. He isn't going to cheat me. I know how to deal with his type."

"Good, because you seem like the persistent type, especially with that much money involved. I don't think you'd let Chad Livingston outsmart you." After a moment he added, "I guess this is goodbye."

Curt replied, "Goodbye and good riddance — as long as you're telling me the truth."

"Check it out. I'm telling the truth."

Cane smirked and watched Curt walk away as he heard him say to himself, "Chad Livingston. Yeah, I can't wait to talk to him."

CHAPTER 13

six months later

Cane found himself staring in the mirror, wondering if he was doing the right thing. His stomach was churning as if he'd been on a roller coaster and he'd just eaten an entire greasy pizza. There was a knock at the door and a voice from the other side that said, "Mr. Cane? Are you ready? It's time."

Cane took a deep breath to ease his fears. He took one last look in the mirror and said to himself, "This is it. This is what you've been waiting for. Calm down and be a man and get out there." Then he replied, "I'll be right out."

The next few minutes were a blur. He found himself on a beautiful beach, standing next to Lindsey. A voice asked, "Lindsey, do you take Wendell to be your lawfully wedded husband, to love and to cherish, in sickness and in health, until death do you part?"

Cane felt a lump in his throat and took a big gulp for air as he awaited her answer. Lindsey said, "I do."

"Wendell, do you take Lindsey to be your lawfully wedded wife, to love and to cherish, in sickness and in health, until death do you part?"

Cane looked into Lindsey's eyes. She was the most beautiful thing he had ever seen in his life. He didn't hesitate a moment. "I do."

The minister smiled and said, "By the power vested in me, I now pronounce you husband and wife. You may kiss the bride."

Cane immediately kissed Lindsey as the small group of onlookers clapped. Lindsey said, "I love you, Mr. Cane."

Cane's face lit up; he loved it when Lindsey called him that. "I love you, Mrs. Cane."

Lindsey blushed and smiled at the new name. "Come on, Wendell. Let's go enjoy our reception and the start of our lives together."

At the reception, Cane's best man stood up and said, "A toast! A toast to Lindsey and Wendell! May you live the rest of your lives in happiness together." The group raised their glasses and cheered.

Cane turned to his best man and said, "Thanks, Jim, for being my best man, and thanks especially for being such a good friend."

"No problem," Jim Rankin replied. "After all, you were my best man."

A little later in the evening, Lindsey said to Jim, "So what did really happen with you and how did you fake your death."

"Yeah Jim, Lindsey never did hear how it all came down," Cane added.

Jim kissed his wife, Anita, took a deep breath and began, "I knew my life was going nowhere and that I had never really done anything of significant value. I was a drone in society, lost without a cause. I was sick and tired of everyone always pushing me around.

"When I saw Doris Catrell come up to my counter at the store I thought, *Oh no, not again. I'm going to be her patsy and give in to her like I always do.* But when she started getting nasty with me, I just snapped. For thirty years I had taken all the world had given me, and I finally broke. Afterward, I felt great. It was like the weight of the world had been lifted off my shoulders.

"Almost immediately after I was fired, things started happening for me. People treated me differently. I realized it wasn't them; it was me. Since I had changed, I was making my own luck and I knew it.

"I realized I had wasted my whole life and I was bitter about it. I started thinking about how to get revenge on everyone who had made my life miserable all those years. It would be impossible to get them all back personally, so I figured I'd get society as a whole. But how could I do it? I wanted to devise a plan to at least get back as many people as I could even if it was in a small way. Then I had an idea — I would take out a five million dollar life insurance policy and fake my death. I struggled with it for a while and realized that if I did fake my death, it would only get society back in a small way because of higher insurance premiums as a whole. It wasn't the best way to get revenge, but I figured it was better then nothing. And it sounded great, possibly getting five million on top of it.

"Then one night I went to this bar where Rachelle was my favorite dancer. When I saw her, I got the idea. I would make Rachelle the beneficiary on a huge insurance policy after asking her to marry me. I did a little research on her and found out she'd been a user her entire life, manipulating people, especially men. She was the exact type of person I wanted to get back at for the thirty years of abuse I'd experienced.

"I knew it would be easy to get her to say yes to my proposal; she was in terrible debt from her wild lifestyle and wouldn't be able to resist the opportunity. I also told her that even if it didn't work out, we could get a divorce and she'd get half my money. It was the perfect setup; she'd win no matter what. So I bought an engagement ring and told her I wanted to marry her, and she said yes. She was consumed with greed.

"I knew the plan was working perfectly when I overheard her telling another dancer that she was going to marry me, get a divorce, and take me for everything I had. That day I knew I could string her along as long as I had to. The thing she didn't know about was the insurance policy. I had her sign so many papers, she didn't know what was going on.

"The first part of my plan was set. But how could I stage my death and get away with it? Well, one day I was at a bar, having a drink and minding my business, when two huge men came in. They looked around and saw this other guy at the bar, and walked up to him and grabbed him.

"He was no match for the big guys. They pushed him up against the wall and said, 'You owe Mr. J. twenty big ones, and he wants it now.' The man said, 'I don't have it now, but I'll have it by the end of the week.'

"One of the guys took him by the throat and said, 'You'd better have it by the end of the week or we're going to come down to your office and visit you, Dr. Hutchinson.'"

"I watched as the big man clenched his hand around the doctor's throat and said, 'You have until Friday, or it's twenty-five thousand. Got it?' The doctor said, 'I got it.' And the big guy let go and actually brushed off the doctor's clothes, as if he was being considerate or something.

"As the two guys were leaving, the one who'd had his hand around the doctor's neck said, 'Three o'clock Friday. And I wouldn't try to avoid us if I were you. I can guarantee Mr. J. wouldn't be happy and we'd have to teach you some manners about being polite and punctual.' The doctor said, 'You'll have it. Don't worry.'

"After they left, the doctor finished his drink, threw a tip on the bar, and walked out. Intrigued by everything that had happened, I followed him to his car and said, 'I couldn't help but notice those two guys who threatened you.' The doctor said, 'It's none of your business what I do. Leave me alone and get out of here.'

"I said, 'Maybe I can help you.' The man said, 'Really? And how's that? If you don't have twenty grand then you can't help me one bit.' But I had just gotten my severance pay and I would gladly give him twenty grand if he was actually a medical doctor who could help me with my plan.

I said, 'I just might be able to throw twenty grand your way if the situation is right.'

"The doctor said, 'What's this all about?' I asked him about himself and found out he was the coroner at the county morgue. I couldn't believe my luck. It was exactly what I needed, someone to pronounce me dead to fool the insurance company. I quickly told him my plan.

"Dr. Hutchinson didn't want any part of it at first because he said it was unethical. I asked how a person who bets thousands of dollars illegally could be so concerned with ethics, and reminded him that his friends were going to come see him again on Friday. He asked what his stake in it was and I told him I'd give him twenty thousand dollars up front and five hundred thousand when I got the insurance money. He changed his mind really fast. We came to an agreement and he helped me plan the whole thing after that.

"First of all, he told me that there was a type of poison from a frog in South America, which, if it was administered correctly, would make me appear to be dead, but actually I'd be in a hibernation state. Only with a complete and thorough examination and detailed testing could an experienced physician tell I wasn't dead. My heart would beat faintly about five times a minute. He said the key was to get just the right amount of the poison, or I could die.

"Dr. Hutchinson told me that the Amazonian red spotted frog's poison was extremely rare and illegal in the United States and that the only place I could get it was Argentina. So I was off to Argentina on my quest to find one of the rarest poisons in the world.

"When I got down here, I absolutely fell in love with this place. It was gorgeous, and the weather was perfect; I felt like I was in paradise and never wanted to leave. After a week of searching, I finally found a source for the poison, and let me tell you, it wasn't cheap. I had to bring back enough so Dr. Hutchinson could experiment to find precisely how much I should take. He's actually brilliant; he discovered the exact amount after only a few days."

Cane interjected, "That explains why he was so picky about everything. I mean, I just thought he was weird. I guess the fact that he was so precise with all his times about cooking food paid off for you. He was obviously a fanatic about being exact."

Jim said, "Well, it's a good thing for me he was so precise or I could've been dead from too much of the toxin. Anyway, when I got back, I set up a bank account in my name and Rachelle's, where the funds would be transferred if I died. And again, Rachelle had no idea about the account. I simply had her sign the papers without looking at them. I got a good attorney to be the executor of my will. I made sure that Rachelle did get the bulk of my tangible assets to throw her off about the account. If she didn't get some money up front, she might have pestered the insurance company too much and found out about the offshore account.

"After that, I had to stage my death in a public place where it would take a little time for me to get to the hospital. I had to leave plenty of time for the toxin to take effect. I figured an office building during the morning rush would be perfect, and the hospital was always busy then because of accidents and what have you. So the stage was set and I had it perfectly planned.

"I took the toxin ten minutes before my job interview. I remember feeling a little faint at the reception desk and then I don't remember a thing. I guess I went into County as a DOA. The next thing I remember was Dr. Hutchinson shaking me and saying, 'Jim, get up.'

"I changed my clothes, sneaked out of the morgue, and flew to Argentina and waited. In the meantime, Dr. Hutchinson prepared everything meticulously. He sent a John Doe body to the funeral home and requested immediate cremation. He prepared bogus blood samples, and of course the toxicology report came back perfect. He fixed that up and wrote the phony autopsy report."

"I was just another heart attack victim as far as Philadelphia Mutual was concerned. I mean, who was going to question Dr. Hutchinson? It was the perfect plan. There was a death certificate, I died in a public place, the coroner had a meticulous report, and I was out of the country. What could go wrong? The one thing that I didn't count on was Wendell Cane."

"Yes, that's where I came in," said Cane." "From the beginning the case stunk and I thought there had to be fraud involved somewhere. I had a thirty-year-old's death in which the money was supposed to be transferred overseas, into an account of someone the person had known for six months. I thought this one would be easy to prove.

"I soon realized how wrong that was. I had a report that said Jim died of a heart attack. I had a beneficiary who was undeserving but seemed legitimate. I struggled; every time I tried to follow a lead it came up false. I kept digging and digging and still I had nothing but a bunch of messed-up, greedy people who were willing to cut each other's throats for that money.

"I was almost ready to give up that day I went to Jim's apartment. I knew there had to be something missing, so I bribed his manager to let me in. That cost me a hundred and fifty bucks! It seemed a bit excessive at the time."

Jim laughed. "Like you need to worry about a hundred and fifty bucks."

"Well, it was a lot of money to me then," Cane continued. "Anyway, I dug around your apartment for a while and found a credit card statement and a receipt. And sure enough, there it was, as plain as day: a receipt for a round-trip ticket to Argentina. Right then I knew something was going on. An offshore account plus a round trip ticket to Argentina equaled a big red flag. So I researched your trip and found you used an alias. It suddenly all started making sense. By the way, your forged passport was brilliant, Jim."

Jim just smiled and said, "Thank you."

"I figured Rachelle was in on it with Jim and he was going to meet her here after she collected the money," Cane continued. But then with Curt involved, I had doubts about her and wasn't sure how it was going to work. And there was still the signed death certificate and coroner's report. I suspected the coroner was on the take after hearing him on the phone to his bookie; I knew he was desperate. Everything changed when I heard my boss talking about laying me off. All of a sudden my loyalty to Philadelphia Mutual was gone. I still can't believe they did that to me.

"Anyway, after that I had no choice but to fly down to Argentina and try to find Jim. I knew Philadelphia Mutual had no power over him even if I did find him. I knew that Argentina has no extradition to the U.S. for crimes, especially in just a fraud case, so I wasn't sure what I intended to accomplish. Then I thought, if I could find him, he'd have no choice but to make a deal if he wanted to get the money. So when I got down to Argentina, I hired an investigator to find him.

"When I returned to the U.S., I had two little obstacles to conquer. I had to get Livingston to sign the settlement and I had to get Accounting to process it without flagging such a large payout. I went into Livingston's office and he simply signed the form without even looking at it. All he cared about that day was his golf game, and he got careless. It was easy.

"I went to Lindsey, who worked in Accounting and could process the claim. I explained how she was going to be let go and how, if she did this for me, we could move to Argentina together. I figured that if Jim wouldn't make a deal, I'd just withdraw the claim. After Lindsey agreed, it was just a matter of waiting. Of course, it didn't hurt any that I fell in love with her in the process."

Lindsey said, "Oh, Wendell," and gave him a kiss. Then she said, "Hey! I did nothing wrong. All I did was process a claim that was signed by the president and CEO of our company. I was just doing my job."

"I know, dear. You're one hundred percent exonerated from any wrongdoing," said Cane, and went on, "I figured it would take a while to find Jim. The investigator finally called a few days after I got back to the States and said that he had located him. I flew back down and hired two big bodyguards to escort me while I approached him."

Cane turned to Jim. "When I went up to you and said 'Jim, Jim, I know it's you,' I'll never forget the surprised look on your face. I mean, to see me catch up with you from halfway around the world must have been amazing. And when you denied who you were, you looked ridiculous. I knew it was you. Oh, by the way, those bodyguards wouldn't have done a thing. They were there just to intimidate you, and I guess it worked.

"Anyway, I told Jim what Philadelphia Mutual did to me. I made him the proposition that if I made sure the payout went through, he would give me one million dollars. Jim, not really having any recourse, had to agree to it or he wouldn't get anything. So we shook on it. I also took the precaution of setting up an offshore account and reminded him that even though there was no extradition in Argentina, my company would go to the ends of the earth to get the money back if he didn't put my share in my account and I reported fraud. He had no choice but to go through with it. I called Lindsey after that and told her to send the claim through. Next I flew back to the U.S.

"A few days later, the check cleared and was put into Rachelle's and Jim's account. Jim had thought of everything, sending the money to six different countries in different accounts and then here, so it wouldn't be traceable. Even if Rachelle could find out where the money started out, she could never trace the transfers to the other banks."

"I checked my account every day knowing he had to be true to his word and transfer the one million dollars to me. It was a waiting game from there. When Livingston called me to his office that last day, I knew exactly what it was about. It was worth it just to see his face when he found out that check had already cleared.

"Lindsey and I were both laid off and unemployed, but we got nice settlements, and plenty to live on down here for the rest of our lives. You can buy a house down here for twenty thousand and live like a king for a lifetime on the severance we got. It was well over three hundred thousand in all."

Jim said, "And you still have the one million from me, Wendell."

"I know, but I don't think I'm ever going to touch that money," Cane said. "The three hundred thousand plus is enough for us. We have each other and we don't really need any more. Besides, it was enough just to see Livingston's face when he found out he'd lost. The money isn't important. And I know it would be wrong for me to touch that money. I spent twenty years preventing fraud and I don't think I could spend it and live with myself."

"I know what you mean," Jim said. "I haven't really touched the money, either. I'm just happy to be here with my new wife, Anita. She is everything that I could have ever hoped for, and more." Anita smiled.

"The way I see it," said Cane, "Philadelphia Mutual got what they deserved for cheating so many people over the years. So what if they had to pay out one false claim? Livingston still got his money. Jim, do you ever feel bad for Rachelle?"

"No way. She got over eighty thousand dollars from my estate; not bad considering she was going to cheat me anyway if I married her. She would have still been broke, even if she did get the five million. People like her will never have money; no matter how much they get, they'll always spend more than they have. Besides, after she used so many people in her life and after so many people used me, how could I feel bad for her?

"I don't feel bad for anyone. Bridget was a miserable person anyway; she should have gone to prison on that conspiracy charge and she didn't. Seth's still with his wife and hating it. Curt ended up with Rachelle; that relationship is doomed, but on the other hand, they're perfect for each other. They get what they deserve."

Jim paused to reflect. "I guess I do feel a little guilty for taking the money from Philadelphia Mutual. I know it was wrong. I know I'll never be able to go back to The United States. It was my home for thirty years. And as much as I disliked my brother, he is family and I'll never see him again. Plus, whenever you do anything wrong like this, it comes with severe consequences. I'm going to have to always be looking over my shoulder wondering if anyone is watching me. It's a heavy price to pay."

"Don't you dare feel guilty," Cane said. "I saved them millions over the years. You have three and a half million after you paid off the coroner and me. Just don't think about it. Enjoy your lovely wife and your new life."

Cane tried to change the subject, laughed and added, "You know, Curt ended up eventually being forced to take anger management classes because he drove himself to the brink by constantly harassing Livingston. Curt actually believed it was Livingston who cheated him. Livingston eventually had to get a restraining order against Curt. After that, he retired with probably three to four million, then his wife left him and took half of everything he had. That served him right."

"What about Dr. Hutchinson?" Lindsey asked.

"Oh yeah, Hutchinson. I transferred half a million into his account. He did his job and I honored our deal. He said he was going to quit gambling and go to Gambler's Anonymous. Somehow I think he'll never be able to quit, though."

Jim looked around and added, "You know, if you had told me two years ago I'd be living in the most beautiful place in the world, with the most beautiful woman in the world by my side as my wife, I would've said you were crazy."

"Me, too," said Cane. Both Cane and Jim looked into their wives' eyes; each husband kissed his new wife.

Cane said, "Jim, I want to thank you and Anita again. I never thought I would have friends like you in my life."

"Right back at you, buddy."

Cane looked thoughtful. "Is there anything about your old life that you miss?"

"Not much," said Jim. "My life was pretty miserable for the most part before I came here. The only thing I really miss is Brian. He was a great friend and a great guy. Somehow, though, I think he'll be fine."

Cane turned to Lindsey and said, "What about you? Do you miss anything about your old life?"

Lindsey didn't hesitate. "Not one thing. What about you, Wendell?"

Cane thought for a moment and said, "As a matter of fact, there is. I miss my pet mice. Every time things got bad I could unwind by spending time with them. They were really cool. I had to give them away when we came here. I bet they miss me. You know, I miss not having a pet. I think I'm going to go out and get me one."

Everyone's eyes widened as they looked at Cane. He noticed they were all looking at him strangely and he said, "What? I was thinking about going and getting a dog, not mice!"

Jim, Lindsey, and Anita all breathed a sigh of relief as Lindsey said, "A dog would be perfect for you." Then they all laughed and continued with their celebration long into the night.